HISTORY IS A LIE

Morton R Leader

This book is a work of fiction. Any references to historical events, real people, or real locales are used fictitiously. Other names, characters, places, and incidents are the product of the author's imagination, and any resemblance to actual events or locales or persons, living or dead, is entirely coincidental.

Copyright © 2021 Morton R Leader

All rights reserved.

ISBN: 9798541485271

Chapter One

Year 2000 A.D. – Mach Ville, Kansas State

"We need you, brother. They are burning the flag, our flag, I ain't letting those Motherfuckers do it, I just ain't, man," shouted an agitated Dan down the phone.

"I can't, man. I got the kid, Chantelle is at the hospital still, I can't leave 'til she gets back." Chad checked his watch trying to work out what time he had if any to help Dan out before his wife was expected back, he felt bad, his loyalty divided, he knew that this protest was going to go to shit, and he should have been there but he was also very concerned about his wife's health, she hadn't been too good lately, women's' things, she hadn't divulged any more than that to him, and he hadn't asked.

When the church had said they were going to attend the latest march, protest, or whatever they called it these days, he had known they were out manned. Sure, lots of the ladies said they would go, and some of them could fight, but this really called for the men. When the plan went south, the men were always the ones on the frontline, as much as he wanted to be there he was needed at home today though.

Dan was still pleading, there was desperation in his voice, people were getting hurt, their people, their members and loved ones.

"Okay, okay, enough" Chad submitted. "Town hall, yeah. Ten minutes." He grabbed the baseball bat from next to the front door, picked up the car seat and shouted to his son Billy to put his coat on, they were going out.

Billy was four years old. He was enjoying a happy upbringing in the Eastland branch of the Joseph Baptist Church, totally unaware of the sick views of the flock and his parents." The preacher's extreme world views and ideals were being forced and implanted in his young brain. He put on his over-sized Stars and Stripes jacket his father had given him as he made his way to the car. "Where we going, Daddy?" he asked excitingly as he was strapped into the car seat.

"Daddy just gotta pop into town, that's all," Chad replied in his deep Midwestern accent, "You be a good boy now."

He started the truck up and headed off, wondering what was awaiting him, Dan was a solid guy, could handle himself, the fact he sounded nervous was a worrying sign, time would soon tell what was going down as they joined the freeway.

Gary Symthe-Barlett sat in the back of the van, he hoped

the journey would end soon, the temperature in the van was getting unbearable, the sweat was twofold, heat and nerves. It was starting to become a long day, he sat there with six other men similarly dressed as were the three women that had joined them, black jeans or shorts, combat boots, black unnamed hoodie, no bands, or brands, no message, no details, nothing that could pin-point any one in a large crowd or help out a CCTV operative, this was standard practice now for these types of days out.

These were the rules, the instructions, if you were coming to a protest you had to follow the rules, you may be there for anarchy, but this was organised anarchy, it was all for protection if anything went wrong. Gary was nervous, he was also angry, firstly the row with his mum before leaving was still on his mind, what did she know anyway, life was fine for her in her flashy lawyer job and the big house in the suburbs, she didn't know how privileged she was, she took the money and stayed quiet no matter who she was defending: corrupt politicians, mobster criminals, bent coppers, she didn't care what they had been accursed of, as long as the dollar's came rolling in, turning a blind eye to the plight of the minorities, letting the real struggles pass her by, as long as everything was rosy for her and her clique she didn't care about any injustices there were in the world or even her own country. He hated her, hated everything she stood for, no wonder his dad had left her, Gary was more than happy to donate his trust fund and drop out of Uni to be on the right side of history, yes when he got back home that was what he was going to do, that would show her he thought.

The second thing winding him up was the boring no shows, there was always talk of trouble, the chance of a dust up, he had been promised action, an opportunity to put these racist scum in their place. So far on the previous outings nothing had happened, maybe a kicking for some red neck who had strayed from the path making them easy pickings for Gary and his mates, well more like colleagues than mates, he didn't have too much time for many of them in reality, but this time something had to happen, he needed it to, plus if nothing happened again how would Victoria ever notice him, it was hard enough as they all looked and dressed the same, he couldn't impress her with his flash car, or a weekend at the lake, that wouldn't do at all, no he needed to show her what a hard man he was, how tough he was, how dedicated to the cause he was, he had a special plan today to make sure he would be the talk of the trip back.

He grabbed his rucksack with extra care as they pulled up and parked, he could hear the crowd chanting only a couple of blocks away, maybe today would be the day he had been hoping for.

The town hall was a mere ten-minute drive away. Chad knew that near on twenty of his church members had planned to be there - enough heads, they had thought, to deal with the parade that was planned. However, different groups had obviously turned up to join in, other than just the placard carrying faggots with all their stupid slogans.

He decided to park a little way off the centre and took the time to stand on the step of his pick-up to review the situation. He could see and smell the smoke as it rose above the rainbow flags, the pro-choice banners and other leftist propaganda nonsense. He failed to see any of his group, but the whole area was certainly raucous and chaotic, full of people, there must have been thousands that had turned up, no smoke without fire, and the colour of the plumes meant it was not just a flag or two. This is not good, he thought.

He quickly got back in his truck and decided to drive slowly into the throng to try to find his team. There were people everywhere and as usual the police traitors were doing nothing, just standing around, not even looking menacing at all. In Chad's view it was clear whose side they were on.

He edged the car carefully forward. After about twenty yards of very slow driving, he finally saw his church group in amongst the crowd. It looked like Dan was trying to calmly walk out of the pack, but he was under attack from all sides, people shouting "Nazi, fascist, bastard" at him, as well as some spitting in his direction and jostling him, running in throwing a punch and retreating just as quickly. Dan was one of the "bigger" members of the church, a well-built but stocky lad, like Chad was himself. They had both been in many of these situations before, they knew the score, but what Chad saw worried him. The various black-masked bullies and soy boy aggressors with dyed purple, pink and blue hair were being whipped into a frenzy by a woman with a bull horn, banging out the old tried and tested chants, phones out recording all their heroics as they pushed and taunted anyone in their way. He pulled over into an empty shop courtyard, just on the edge of the action and flashed his lights, hoping Dan would see him.

Billy was sitting in the back and was getting scared by what he could see through his window. He started to cry. Acknowledging this, Chad turned around in his seat to face him, smiled and said, "You be a big, brave boy now for your daddy, I just gonna help Uncle Dan a second."

Dan had seen Chad's car. Thank God, he thought. Chad was right, this had all been a very bad idea; however, the church had still come down with all their usual swagger, their hateful signs made to deliberately provoke people, their chants and songs about how the evil gays are all paedos. The fact that they were so over the top usually kept them safe. People either thought they were just so stupid they moved on as fast as possible not giving them the attention they so obviously craved, or, as they were so in your face and provocative, normal folk thought that there was no line these nutters wouldn't cross, so they steered well clear. Perhaps it was due to not enough of the men turning up this time to impose themselves properly, to make a stand. Nine of the sixteen members that had made an appearance were women, four of them were in their sixties and although these old timers were full of attitude they weren't as fit and agile as they used to be, their minds were willing, but their bodies were letting them down. With these odds the deviants fancied their chances today.

Gary had been looking for trouble and opportunity all day. Where's he heading to? he thought as he spotted one of the church weirdos making his way out of the crowd, escaping, a big bloke who had been making his presence known all day. Oh no he doesn't. Not if I have anything to do with it.

Gary was finally happy; he had come along with a crowd of like-minded people hoping that these idiots would turn up and try to start something. He and his antifascist mates had come down from Chicago for that reason alone. When big-city boys come to small-town America, there is only going to be one winner, he thought smugly. He had been to three previous rallies and was disappointed that they were relatively peaceful, and nothing had happened; he was promised some action and the chance to beat up Nazis when he signed up. This time, fuck it, he was going to stake his claim as a bad ass and show these people not to mess with him. He knew if he got in trouble the team had his back, if he was isolated the women would arrive and act as peace makers, make out they were furious with him for starting trouble whilst all the time saving him for getting hurt, a human shield of sorts, it was a good tactic that fooled anyone filming. He spotted the big bloke heading towards a pickup.

He's not getting away, he thought, and backed off a little out of the main group so he could get to his rucksack.

Seeing that Dan was starting to get even more battered, the scum getting braver and braver as he retreated, Chad got out of the pickup, hoping his size wouldn't go unnoticed. At six foot five, he towered above nearly all the crowd and his face told a don't-fuck-with-me story. Having said that, the odds were heavily against them; sheer numbers always counted in the end, it only took one slip to find yourself on the deck, once there the jackal's would sense blood and home in for the kill, kicking you on the ground, one on one Chad was more than a match for anyone, but this was a braying, nasty intent group, he had been around long enough to know that, plus he had been on the other side as well and knew how these things worked.

The booing, chanting, spitting and name calling intensified as they came together. Chad put his arm around Dan and hurried him towards the car, taking him to the passenger side first. He noticed Dan had a bloody nose and a cut on his forehead. He pushed his way around to the driver's side, having to punch out some pink-haired screaming banshee woman; her bravery enhanced by the crowd and the knowledge that she had been brought up with that men shouldn't hit women. She totally misread the situation as she was felled in one hit from the massive man, she was lucky though in one way, as normally he would have ensured she wasn't able to get back up, he hoped his sign to anyone else that fancied messing with him was understood now, but today this crowd was not happy and was already baying for revenge blood, it was all getting too violent to hang around any longer than he had to.

"You okay?" Chad shouted above the noise as he got into the pickup. He hit the central locking and revved the engine, hoping to split the crowd. Hopefully punching that cow had shown he meant business. Dan just nodded, he looked totally despondent, beaten down, the young Billy was still sobbing in the back.

Chad jumped the pickup forward as a warning, over revving the engine on purpose. The crowd in front made a small gap, not wanting to get run over, despite the calls to stand their ground from the ring leaders at the back, just like the generals of old. The front was good news, but the sides were taking a pounding, fists, placards and some wooden stakes were being used. He revved the engine again, the powerful 5.7 litre growling away as it moved forward with better effect. The crowd in the front seemed to realise that this guy did indeed mean business; perhaps some felt that having them run away was the best result. Just as Chad sped up, the two back windows were smashed in, showering Billy in broken glass shards, causing him to bellow and become further upset, his young eyes darting around full of terror, shaking his head side to side, now screaming loudly. Chad looked over his shoulder quickly and saw that no real injury had occurred, thank God, but his mind was focused now on getting the hell out of there, he couldn't put his child at any more risk, this was not going well!. He quickly turned back to the wheel to see if the gap was now big enough for him to drive through, he guessed it would do as he gunned the pedal. If he had misjudged it, well, that was their fault.

Gary knew he had one good chance left, he looked around to see if Victoria was anywhere near as it seemed the vile pigs were getting away, he didn't want to lose his chance to impress her. After lighting it he hurled his homemade Molotov cocktail with all his might. It sailed through the air, hitting the Dodge on the frame of the already busted back window, bursting into flames as it did so, the fiery sticky liquid spilled into the car and a child's scream cut through the noise of the crowds. Gary was taken aback by the explosion, he stood frozen suddenly concerned about his actions, Victoria appeared from the panicked and quickly dispersing crowd, she grabbed his arm and ushered him along as they dived further into the larger crowd back towards the town centre, the lack of colour clothes adding to the camouflage of the throng, she knew she needed to get Gary out of there as fast as she could.

Chapter Two

2019 AD – Las Vegas

FBI Special Agent Adam "The Edge" Clayton waved to the uniformed cop as he passed through the police line and parked the sedan opposite the latest crime scene in what was now becoming a very serious affair.

It was always warm in the desert in the day time, even at this time of year, not like back in his home state of Illinois, the winters there could be so unforgiving, the Christmas trees and decorations donning the streets back there were great, here right now looking odd and out of place in such a warm climate. Adam was dressed in a suit and tie, complete with jacket though, it was important to him to look professional, look the part, not only act it, he knew some of his colleagues would be wearing short sleeved shirts, some would even be wearing shorts, it wasn't right in his view.

As he quickly looked around the area, his mind taking it all in, he confirmed it was the same sort of location as previous scenes: a night-by-night rented chalet on the outskirts of town, a frequent hang-out for all sorts of low life's, druggies, dealers, pimps and hookers. No one ever mentioned the good honest people that supported these networks, the ones that kept all of them in business. No, it was all the providers' fault. He hated that the policy was to stop the supply, not the demand. If he ever got to where he wanted to be in the organisation, a top position in power, he promised himself he would do his best to alter that tact. Yep, you could find all the scum of the earth in these places; users and providers; to Adam they were just two sides of the same coin, all could be found and seen here.

"Hey here's The Edge," shouted Tony Lopez warmly, not only a fellow investigator but a friend as well. Adam was nicknamed The Edge for two reasons – the silly one and the work one – the silly one being when he first introduced himself and, being a music fan, he made the mistake of saying, "Adam Clayton, same as the man in U2," to which someone innocently and incorrectly shouted, "Oh, the Edge!" Strangely, that was enough, and it just stuck, no matter how many times Adam explained that there were two different guitarists in the band. Then, as his reputation grew, the name took on a second meaning. Dedicated to his work, he had the ability to always think of another edge to the story, another arc, things that seemed to be missed by his fellow workers, this ultimately led to him being very good at solving these murders and the like. He had the edge, that was his thing, so, to his team, he became "The

Edge."

Adam was not your stereotypical investigator, with a troubled marriage, a drinking or drugs habit, nor was he coupled up with a working partner who was the complete opposite of him. Adam was a proud family man, with a beautiful wife, Ellen, and two children, Marty, aged six, and Daisy, aged eight – one of each, that was what they had wanted, the perfect family in their view and they were happy it had worked out that way. This stability of his home life, in his mind, was what kept him on his game and drove him to success. The more bad guys he locked up, the safer the world was for not only his loved ones, but the millions of good decent people out there. He truly believed that there were more good people on the planet than bad ones, although his job pushed his reasoning to its limits.

He ducked under the tape and walked in. "What do we have here, then?" he asked no one in particular. In a way, he was asking the open question to himself as he studied the scene in the cheap motel room.

Two dead men, both shot in the groin and head. One victim was slumped in the chair, the other knelt in front of him on the floor with his head in his lap; it looked like the scene had been staged after they had both been killed, with each body being placed in position. Typically, the younger man, being the rent boy, had been shot in the back of the head; the older, shall we say the client, was shot in the forehead, face on.

It was like the perp had wanted to stage what he had

found upon entry into the room, when he most likely caught them in the act itself, Adam guessed.

This was now the third time in three months, in the same sort of area of the states, same MO, same end result. Adam thought, we have a serial killer on our hands now, it's official. The same modus operandi had to be used three times: there had now been six deaths, two at each crime scene.

In Adam's experience, most serial killers were not like they were portrayed in the movies. They had no intricate plan, no weird thing that set them off: Zodiac signs; renting out a certain film; hair colour combined with red shorts. No, most either targeted hookers, the gay community or hitchhikers, with the latter becoming quite rare these days. He couldn't think of the last time he had seen a hitchhiker, never mind been on a case where they were being bumped off. That way of traveling seemed to have vanished from America's highways.

He found through his work and experience that the killers, in his view, were normally driven through pent-up anger, embarrassment and, in a way, how easy and opportunistic the murder could be. These killers didn't fit into what was seen as normal homely lives; they were either gay themselves and hated it, felt filthy after having sex with the rent boy or guy they had picked up in a bar, and therefore murdered them to hide their shame, or they simply hated gay men as being abhorrent to God in their sick minds, so they killed them.

The same with the hookers: the killer wasn't getting sex

the normal way, so they took their anger out on the poor girl – mostly after having sex, but sometimes before – brutally murdering them. Many never got caught; those perps that did get caught were found before the three-times law, keeping the actual serial killer stats down. It was all about the stats for the men upstairs.

Also, these guys – let's face it, they were all guys – were just cold-blooded killers, strangling, using knives or guns. Again, not like the movies, where they were surgeons or actors, with a skillset anyone would give their right arm for. These fictional "wrong uns" from books or movies knew where to get the needed drugs to knock people out; they were rich; they were strong enough to carry bodies about with ease; they could tie various intricate knots with rope; they had knowledge of Norse myths or Roman gods; they could even dig a grave in permafrost in the middle of winter! All the while masking it, hiding their lifestyle from any family, loved ones and work colleagues. It was all bullshit, thought Adam, although he had to admit it made for better films. The real ones just trapped or followed the target and butchered them. This one obviously had a gun, and once you point a gun at someone, you would be surprised what you can make them do.

Adam was thinking hard as he stood there, the forensics teams doing their bit, when Tony piped up: "Oh shit, that's Chucky Wallback." He was pointing to the tall, well-built, athletic looking man in the chair.

Adam looked. It had been hard to see upon first inspection, with the blood and the skull shattered from the bullet hole, but Tony was right: that was old Chucky, the LA Lakers number one-point guard. I guess he wasn't such a straight-up all-American red-blooded male, the all-round family good guy after all, Adam thought.

This wasn't good. Confirmed serial killer with three crime scenes and six murders under his belt in a short three months, and now a famous well-known victim. The lads on the team had already started to refer to the case as that of the Dickhead Killer, as each of the victims were shot once in the genitals and once in the head. Due to lack of movement of the bodies, the forensics thought he had the men resume their position of the sex act they were performing this time, or the killer had caught them in the act, he then shot the one performing the act in the back of the head before immediately shooting the receiver. He finished off by shooting both men in the groin – well, penis area, to be precise. The press was going to have a field day with this. Adam just hoped they would come up with a better name than his colleagues had.

For now, he had seen all he needed to. The time spent at the other two sites had given him enough to go on; there didn't seem to be anything new here. The team already had the local force check for CCTV in the area, the officers were already checking the other chalets, interviewing to see if anyone had seen or heard anything, noticed anything, all normal protocol was in place and would be sent to him once finished. It was time for The Edge to do his stuff, and he returned to the office to hammer the databases.

As the chosen files downloaded, back at the office, he set his thoughts out using old-fashioned paper and pencil. What did we know? Local area. Obviously had it in for homosexuals. Used a gun. Did he have an issue with rent boys in particular, the client that was paying for it, or both? Was the shooting of the actual penis important? He made some swirling patterns on the paper, jotting down his different thoughts, he had sat there mulling it over for two hours as he waited for the information from the local boys to come through.

The Edge was feeling good, a little smug even, three suspects had been ruled out already as two were back inside and one was now dead. This was a great help and made his work a lot easier as he had decided that this was about revenge and punishment, he was beginning to get a really good feeling about this one now. He was sure that there was something in the killer's past that had triggered off these murders, something to do with gays; had he been touched up, molested or raped? Whatever it was, he appeared to hate them, therefore he wanted to kill them and shoot their penises off. This was the route Adam would go down for now, until evidence came up that proved him wrong and sent him in a different direction. With the database now fully downloaded, he started to filter on his assumptions and building in the facts coming back from the crime scene. He further reduced the suspects down to a manageable workload.

The CCTV footage showed that a hire car had been parked in the parking lot of the motel, Adam remembered that there had been reports of a hire car at the previous two locations as well, this in itself was not too unusual as hire cars in motel areas was the norm, however there had been a report recently of the same make of car driving on the wrong side of the road near Boulder City, was this a link, was it relevant to the case, food for thought he surmised, did this rental car mean anything?

Chapter Three

2019 AD – Las Vegas

William, as he now called himself, kept his distance from his new target, not wanting to be seen. He wasn't worried though, he was getting good at this now, with three successful hits under his belt, plus a home invasion that turned out a bit messier than he had planned, however he felt confident, but also knowing, now wasn't the time to get cocky. No need to take risks when there were so many – so, so many – targets. For people that couldn't reproduce as God intended, there did seem to be an awful lot of them, especially in this godforsaken city. Anyway, he congratulated himself, six less, thanks to him – soon to be eight.

    He had returned to the States nine months ago and he was shocked to see the horrific decline of his country, he wasn't stupid nor had been living in a bubble, but he didn't expect the amount of blatant debauchery. The open gayness was awful. Gay pride month – a whole month! He couldn't believe it, rainbows everywhere, TV and radio stations either fronted by a pervert or the programmes full of them, news articles about how great they were, such a fabulous lifestyle choice, all so stunning and brave. They were even letting them in the army these days. How would they protect the country? In his mind it was ridiculous. All this, whilst good honest God-fearing folk were being picked upon. It seemed the USA, just like the UK which he had recently left, had a world order: gays at the top and everyone else shat on; gays' beliefs trumped anyone else's. Then there was the battle for religion, with Islam trumping Christianity, in a Christian country! This was insane. With what the homos had done to him, they were going to pay, all of them.

He had spent two years of his young life in hospital in the UK. He had been flown there as soon as he was stable, a young pioneering doctor was trying new techniques for burn cases such as his, it suited the authorities in the USA as they wanted to distance themselves from the incident and were therefore more than happy to send the injured child overseas. He'd had no visitors, as his mum and dad had been arrested in what was known as the Mach Ville massacre. After the petrol bomb had hit the car, his dad and gone nuts, putting his foot down hard on the accelerator and driving at the crowd, killing one of the protestors and seriously injuring seven others. It was total chaos, but the media had focused on his church and the only person arrested and imprisoned was his dad. His frustration at being taken away from his injured son and not knowing how he was, led Chad to take his anger out on anyone who got in his way, this consequently led to him being ganged up on and killed during a fight with a fellow inmate, to which the guards seemed to turn a blind eye to.

The police arrested a couple of suspects for the attack on the car and throwing the bomb but there were no eyewitnesses and not enough evidence for a trial once the lawyers had gotten involved. No other charges were made, even though a four-year-old was seriously burnt and disfigured for life. His mother, although not at the event, was arrested four days later as she took a gun into town to a gay bar to exact revenge. She didn't get a round off as she was on a watch list and being followed. She was then totally stitched up and also sent to prison, she passed away from cancer just three months later.

The establishment had wanted to finish this church, it was as simple as that, the TV documentary was the final straw , it had been an embarrassment of the town for way too long, they investigated every angle from finance to child abuse and gun ownership, all the major players ended up in jail on trumped-up charges, there was no one left to care for poor little Billy, who by now was thousands of miles away.

Thankfully, the burning liquid thrown that fateful night had not hit his face. This was the only good news. His young body took the full force and his genitals had to be removed soon after, leaving Billy having to urinate through a tube. His body would always be in pain, from his chest down to his knees, and as he grew he would have to have more and more surgery to cut his body, as his skin would not stretch properly.

These further operations were all completed in England, where he was eventually adopted by a nice family, Henry and Ruth. Henry had a career in medicine, whilst Ruth worked in law; these roles combined ensured they were more than comfortably well off, with a genuine desire to help this poor innocent child. Due to the nature of the injuries and the downfall of the church, a new start away from Mach Ville was considered to be the best option, with a different country seen as a perfect setting, a new chance for this severely physically as well as mentally damaged child.

They had been good loving parents, and they did their best for William, as they now called him. He was bright and gained a good education in school before going to university, where he studied for a degree in history. William tried his best to move on, and it worked quite well initially. He made a huge effort to forget his first four years of indoctrinated hate in the church, the next two years of constant pain and operations, but sadly, when puberty kicked in, the memories resurfaced as the frustration of his deformity came to the fore.

He was clever enough to keep these feelings hidden, not only from his adopted parents, but also from the counsellor that he had always had since moving to the UK. But inside it ate away at his soul. These sinners, these filthy dirty degenerate perverts were fucking each other and sticking their penises God knows where else, and it was an affront to the Almighty Himself, whilst he...yes, he didn't even have a penis with which to do what God intended and recreate! He would never know the joy of being a father – hell, he would never bed a woman, or even have a relationship or have the chance to carry on his family name.

He decided at fourteen what he was going to do, what his life calling was. They had made him a freak, they had locked up his parents, they had destroyed his church; they, and by that he meant any homosexual pervert, would pay with their life.

William was now stalking Liam. Liam was a rent boy he had viewed online to find his next victim – yep, he would do – another little gay boy, soon to be a dead little gay boy.

Liam was totally unaware he was being followed. He was concentrating on the instructions he had been given. They were a bit more intense than normal, but then again, so was the money, and that didn't hurt, being three times his usual rate. That would do very nicely. He could call it a night after this one. Perhaps the client was famous or someone high up in the government. Most of his clients were like that – men's men, big gruff hard men, professional sports stars or tough-guy actors – people no one would guess liked getting their cock sucked by a slight-of-frame, five-foot-four feminine gay guy, but it was what it was and happened more often than not.

Liam had been a rent boy since he was twenty, once he found out his fondness for these casual encounters could make him money; he'd been doing it for free in many of the gay bars around Vegas as he partied his way through his teens anyway. This money paid his bills and let him enjoy the life he led when not working. So, what if he had to suck off some old men who he wouldn't normally? Perhaps his dad was right when he kicked him out all those years ago: he was nothing more than a filthy little faggot, cock sucker, but this was where he had found himself and, although he didn't think he would do it forever, he was surprised he had been doing it now for nearly eight years.

Speaking of finding himself, he thought he recognised this area. Had he been here before? Was this a repeater? His mind was unclear, but he couldn't shake the thought that this place was familiar. Oh well, he thought. So many cocks, so many motels; perhaps I did such a good job last time, he wants more. He smiled to himself as he found the right chalet.

William saw Liam tap on the door and enter; he didn't quite get a look at who had answered. Never mind. He was confident with his plan. After all, it was becoming old hat now he was three times in, quite the expert.

He took the pistol out of the glovebox of his rental car and checked the bullets, pulled on his black latex gloves and took his key set. As always, he waited, planning the events in the chalet out in his head. Let them relax and get going. To be fair, it didn't usually take long before they were at it, so he counted to three hundred before leaving his rented car. The hunter was circling his prey.

The hunter didn't know he himself was also being stalked. His hire car had been placed on a watch list by the FBI, a patrol car driving pass had spotted it parked in the area, the officer did a U turn, stopped and was about to have a quick look around to see if she could see who was driving it, or where the driver was, she hadn't seen anything out of the ordinary when she had driven past, however, a crash five miles away had disturbed her investigation so she had just called it in and gone about her business.

Adam was sat at his desk when the information came through, had he lucked out that quickly? He had chased his hunch; after checking history records, car rentals, as well as flight records, he'd come across this suspect. This guy certainly had reason, from what he had read of the case, the poor sod. He'd also returned to the US just a few months before the time of the first killing. Was this too good to be true? Had "The Edge" got it in one? If it was this easy, perhaps the Dickhead name allocated by the team was spot on, as he was leaving plenty of clues, like forgetting which side of the road you should be on in America, this little incident stood out for an experienced investigator like Adam.

Don't get carried away, his inner ego cautioned, you have nothing yet. Just hang fire and see what might develop.

He was about to make his way to the destination when his wife Ellen called, a short chat followed as she wished him luck on his latest case, she herself was taking the children to see her mum back home in Chicago for the weekend, he couldn't quite place it then but something resonated in his brain, Chicago, Chicago, why did that seem relevant?.

William cautiously listened at the door. No noise, he confirmed. No talking, perhaps they were already underway in their deviant act. He expertly picked the cheap, crappy lock – only an expert in his own mind, since a small child with a paper clip could open most doors in these places.

He entered the room at speed, hoping to catch out any occupants. As he quickly scanned the room to get his bearings, he couldn't believe the sight that greeted his eyes. Wow – he did not see that coming.

Chapter Four

2019 AD – Las Vegas

Marcus stood in the doorway that led from the lounge area of the chalet to the small kitchen and bathroom, a now empty pint glass in his hand, stained with blood. He heard a slight noise just before the door sprang open to reveal this man in a trench coat. The long leather trench coat standing out in the Vegas heat, even at this time of the year it was still hot, Marcus then spotted the gun in his outstretched hand pointed at him, Marcus was too long in the tooth to be surprised and certainly if he was indeed shocked by the intruder he didn't show it.

Both men looked at each other as time froze for a minute, they both looked towards the silent docile Liam. William noticed he was sitting in a chair, his eyes wide open, mouth agape, a completely blank expression on his face, as if in some sort of trance – hypnotised, if you like. As William's gaze went down Liam's body, he noticed his sleeve was rolled up and he had some sort of makeshift medical device attached to his arm, slowly dripping blood into a bag.

"Come in and shut the door. My name's Marcus," the standing man said in a calm tone, totally alien to the event unfolding before them, almost as if he was commenting on something simple like the weather. He didn't move from where he stood.

Confused and caught off guard, William did as requested, stuttering, "Err . . . William," and nearly extending his own hand, as if wanting this man to shake it.

This wasn't what he was expecting at all. Instead of two perverts engaged in a sick sex act, there was a comatose rent boy with an elderly . . . Well, William wasn't quite sure; at first glance, the man who had introduced himself so nonchalantly, considering the situation they found themselves in, could have been as young as forty or nearing seventy. He was not tall, about five nine at most, slender build, simply dressed in a checked shirt and jeans, slight tan, greyish hair and sparkling youthful blue eyes. Had William happened across another serial killer or some blood fetish player? If killer, then fair enough. What were the chances? But, then again, they were in Vegas, where the whole city worked on chance. If he was a killer, he was not the same ilk as William. This looked weird. What was he doing, or planning on doing, to the rent boy? Why was he in a daze? Was it drugs or had he hypnotised him? If so, how quickly could he do that? Could he be hypnotising William now, just by talking to him? Question upon question swirled around his confused mind.

As if reading his thoughts, Marcus spoke up: "That's Liam, by the way. He's not going to come to any harm. I'm just taking a little more blood." It was true, he hadn't killed anyone in hundreds of years. As he spoke, he swirled the empty glass in his hand. Having just drunk Liam's blood, Marcus believed in his mind he was at the peak of his powers. He scanned William's face for his surface thoughts. "So, you are a killer," he added. "Please, sit down." He was not worried about the gun; sure, a well-placed bullet could kill him, but he had a trick or two to play if needed, and he was confident the blood he had just drunk would increase his magic powers for a while now.

Taking control – after all, he was the one with the gun – William, slightly confused that this man seemed to have already worked out why he was there, the gun a big clue he guessed, instructed Marcus to sit on the sofa, near the chair Liam occupied, while he pulled a chair from the table area. He checked the curtains were well drawn and no gaps were visible. What the hell was going on? Part of him wanted to just bolt out of there, but this was too intriguing. Who was this man? What was he up to? Had he really just drunk this fella's blood?

Both men sat down, William gingerly pointing the revolver at Marcus, Marcus not seeming to care about that one iota.

"You better tell me what's going on," William demanded.

Having no reason to lie and feeling unthreatened, Marcus thought, Why not just tell the truth?, it might be nice to spend some time talking with someone he thought, he had been feeling quite lonely as of late, no beating about the bush, let's have some fun for a change he decided, some company might be nice, after all if it came to it, although it had been a long time, he was sure he could either kill both William and Liam or befuddle them so much they wouldn't know what year it was.

"I needed to feed, as I do every month; sometimes I choose a whore, sometimes a rent boy, I like to mix it up, plus it's good to change supply, keeps me healthy, Liam's his name. He actually is one I've used before, as I know he's clean. I've fed once and was just getting a snack bag's worth when you so rudely came into the room," Marcus stated matter-of-factly, staring directly into Williams eyes.

Ha! He thinks he's a vampire! William laughed in his head, that explains a few things. Here I am, just your common-law serial killer, and I happen across a proper nut job. You couldn't make this up!

"Vampire, eh?" he snorted mockingly. "Oh, please don't turn into a wolf and attack me." William was feeling confident now, the heavy metal killing machine in his hand boosting his confidence. He decided to point it as menacingly as he could to establish who was in charge in the room as he returned the stony stare.

"Well, yes you could say I was a folklore vampire, I

guess," Marcus replied. "Yes, that's what culture and history have decided to push onto us. No thanks for anything else we may have done to you shag-happy chimps." He looked downwards now breaking the eye contact, he seemed almost disappointed in something.

William was unsure what to do. This scenario was never in his wildest plans. He had a complete nutter here in front of him, yet he was quite warming to the guy for some reason. He was sort of charming and his "don't seem to care" nonchalant manner was making William want to know more of what fantasy world Marcus lived in, no harm had been done so far so there was nothing to particularly worry about for the time being, maybe he could learn something from this man, not folklore and myths but about killing people and getting away with it.

"Go on then," he said. "Enlighten me, oh wise one."

Marcus could detect the sarcasm in William's voice. It had been a while – too long, really – since he had had a really-good chat with anyone, not just his own kind but anyone at all. William did seem like an interesting person, what with the serial-killer thing he had going on. These days he only really chatted to the dealers in the casino's and he always felt that was just part of their job, just meaningless pleasantries, it would take an hour to slow-bleed Liam, and he could always put him under again if needed; the room was booked for twenty-four hours. So, he thought, why not have some company? Might make a nice refreshing change.

"Well, let's clarify some facts first, then I will take you on a journey across history, starting before time itself." Marcus sounded as if he was narrating a play or reading the intro to a movie, but it seemed to have the desired effect on William, who leaned forward to listen. "We, my kind, have always been here, living beside mankind, feeding off you. Your blood not only keeps us alive, but it enhances our powers. We don't have fangs, we can come out in daylight, we can't shapeshift. What else? Err . . . Oh yes, we don't sleep in coffins. No, we just drink your blood, and we are very old – we live for fifty times your lifespan, sometimes more, before we die."

William grinned. Brilliant – he has it well-rehearsed, he thought. Just reeled that off, like reading the back of a book. Was he a movie writer or something? Or an out of work actor, come over from Hollywood to live out his fantasy, you never know, the world was full of weirdo's and America did seem to have more than its fair share.

"So, what on God's earth are you doing here, in a chalet, in Vegas, with a rent boy in a trance? Shouldn't you be in a castle in Europe, or something?" William asked.

"I guess the best place to start is at the beginning, as they say," Marcus suggested, although not many tales in modern-day storytelling did start at the beginning. "Europe, yes – well, eventually."

He took a moment, licked his lips and then began to tell his story to his new unexpected friend.

Chapter Five

330 BC – Greece

Adrian made his way through the camp towards the Colonel's tent perched higher up the hill from the river. He was a fit man, but he was tired from the heat as well as from the efforts earlier. The mood in the camp was jubilant; yet again they had enjoyed success on the battlefield against the Persians. The men were drinking and singing, celebrating their spoils of war.

    The last four years had been very good for the Greeks. At the start, they were dubious on how far they could go, but they swept everyone away in front of them: Gaza; Damascus; Edessa; then the big one, the battle of Gaugamela. Adrian was proud to be a Battalion Leader for such a great leader as Alexander, and now he was the bearer of more wondrous news: an important find, perhaps the most important since the first findings way back in Lydia and Ephesus.

    He passed the sentries posted outside and entered the tent. Before him stood two more Battalion Leaders, one

Colonel, three Brigadiers and the man he had been sent to inform, General Barak. This man reported directly to Alexander.

"Come in, Adrian. Wine?" Barak asked.

Rising from his bowed position, Adrian accepted the wine and took a huge gulp.

"Now, tell me the exciting news."

The Greeks had "found" the first one four years ago, as they had stormed the city. Some troops entered the temple area, the soldiers came across six more guards but in a different uniform to the regular army members. The Greeks had put them quickly to the sword. They seemed to have been designated to protect this room that was based at the back of the temple. Assuming a prince or high-ranking official was inside, perhaps even gold or other riches, they excitedly yet cautiously opened the door. What they found, though, was just a single, unarmed, unassuming man, his only memorable feature was his piercing blue eyes, thus being odd for a Persian, as they all had brown eyes.

Logic said this person was important, so rather than killing him, Adrian's men arrested him and took him to their Leadership on the battlefield. He didn't put up any resistance. As the war continued and each battle unfolded, each city or town sacked, the Greeks came across more of these people behind locked doors – not always men, some were women – of various ages, from perhaps as young as twenty to as old as near on seventy. The Greeks noted the one common feature was the blue eyes, as well as always hidden away, protected by the same dressed guards and always coming peacefully, no resistance.

Adrian's find this time was special, though. This was a family: father, mother, with a teenage daughter and, in the mother's arms, a baby, no more than eighteen months old.

Adrian knew the orders: wipe out the troops, then search for these blue-eyed people; use the unique uniformed guards as a pointer to locate them; do not under any circumstance injure or kill the blue eyes. They had found that they had all come quietly when captured.

They gave them shelter, clothes and got them away from the bulk of the men as soon as possible. They should not talk about it or brag about it, just inform up the ranks as soon as they were successful in the operation. With these four, Adrian reckoned from what he knew himself and what he had heard around the camps the number captured from the Persians was now up to a couple of hundred. He wasn't sure where back home in Greece they were being sent to. He had heard it was a few different places, as the powers wanted them to be kept apart.

Adrian was debriefed and thanked for his work, he was informed that Alexander himself would know of this great find and that it was his troops that had been involved. Adrian felt his chest swell with pride and, as he left the tent, he dreamed of promotion.

Daviid smiled at his wife Ursula, who was sitting opposite him in the covered wagon heading south to Athens.

She had one arm around their daughter Mia, who in turn was holding the baby Marcus. She smiled back. Ursula, like all the blue eyes, knew in her heart that, if they didn't want to be captured, they most likely wouldn't have been, but it had all been agreed.

They had all had enough of the Persians and King Darius. About the same time, the Persians and the Majiksis had learnt their strength and power was in their numbers. If they were separated across distances, their power dwindled. Up until now the Majiksis had not been aware of this, as, for thousands of years, the three main tribes had lived fairly close together.

They had started working in conjunction with the Persians as the human population outside their lands grew and they saw the world around them was slowly changing. The elders were intrigued and wondered how they would fit in this new world and what the future would hold for their people, they decided to set up a sort of partnership with the Persians, helping them create a massive empire. In return, they were treated very well, being indulged in their needs.

As the empire grew, the Persians could see what benefits their new allies had brought, could bring, it was deemed wise to have a Majiksis presence in each city and outpost to help guard and maintain the now massive empire. This was the start of the end. The power of an individual Majiksi, or two or three at the most, couldn't be harnessed as much or as usefully, and therefore it made each city open to attack. The Elders of the Majiksis reviewed the situation and as time went by issued instructions by word of mouth that is was time to explore the further world, to regroup under a new regime. The Greeks were chosen, and that's how now they were slowly reforming and meeting up in a new country, under a new civilisation. The Majiksis would play it differently this time, lessons had to be learnt from their time with the Persians, they were an unknown entity to the Greeks, the true extent of their powers a secret. They wanted to be away from the front lines, away from the battles, the blood and the gore, well aware time as always was on their side, they would use it to their advantage.

Chapter Six

2019 AD – Las Vegas

Marcus finished telling his version of what had transpired those many years ago, he looked over at his captor to see if he could gauge anything on where they now stood or were heading with the situation they had found themselves in, he wanted to see if William was buying into the story or was going to shoot him.

"Wait, wait," William scoffed, hardly containing his laughter. "That's you – Marcus, the baby?" He laughed out loud, he envisioned a dusty old chariot or wagon bumping along a dusty road in Greece, the little baby wobbling about, it made him laugh as he momentarily forgot the situation he was in in this chalet. He regained his composure, quickly, purposefully pointing the gun a little higher, making sure that Marcus was aware of who was in charge here.

Marcus had a sly grin on his face as he replied, "Yes, you wanted the whole story, didn't you?" it seemed he had an audience now, good that was what he wanted he thought.

"So, let me get this straight: that would make you nearly two thousand . . . err . . . two thousand, three hundred odd years old, or something. You live forever?" William asked, quickly checking the maths in his head.

"Not forever, just a lot longer than you. We used to outlive you by fifty times, but just lately you humans have decided to live twice as long as you used to, so maybe not fifty. Perhaps forty plus," Marcus stated, quite factually.

"Okay, okay, just let me get my head around this." William paused to gather his thoughts before continuing. "You come from a tribe of people that look like us, somewhere in the Middle East, you have powers that you used to help the Persians before hooking up with the Greeks when they came with a better offer? What would these magic powers be, then?"

"A mixture. As you can see from our friend Liam here - given time and a calm situation from where to do our magic from - as you can see hypnosis is one of them." Marcus nodded at the trance-like rent boy in the chair, his mind God knows where, as his blood slowly dripped into the makeshift container, he looked happy though, quite content. "Mind control, telekinesis, befuddlement, illusion, some teleportation and, most importantly, we are able to inspire you. Some say we were involved in every major invention in mankind's history, up until the late nineteenth century."

William couldn't argue that Liam looked hypnotised, but then people get hypnotised all the time, don't they? There was a show on right now in Vegas based on it; he bet that act wasn't a fucking vampire!

Gathering his thoughts again, he decided he was going to put this man's story to the test, see if he could catch him out, William struggled with what to ask first. "So, you drink blood then – just human blood? Or animal blood as well?" He was thinking of the films he had seen for inspiration. "And you were born, not made?"

"Yes, it has to be human blood, and – sorry – we are born, just like you. We recreate the same way as any living mammal, we are just another species. Being made, as you call it, is just silly folklore. Think of us like vampire bats: the bat feeds on goats and the like, but the goat doesn't become a bat because it was attacked, a cat doesn't become the flea because the flea drank its blood!"

"But he's gay – his blood, I mean – he could have . . . you know, anything, AIDS or - "

"As I said, he's clean," Marcus interrupted. "I can tell. It's as simple to me as you opening a carton of milk and smelling it to see if it has gone off – it's just the same. If I'm honest, I did have a worry back in the early eighties when that all came about, but we can tell if it's bad blood, cancer, whatever you name it, I can tell."

William decided to go down another track. "You're old, you've been around a long time, you must be bored?" he offered with a hint of sarcasm. Let's see what he comes up with here, if you were really that old what would it be like, what would you do, some people get bored by a Sunday night of a weekend, two thousand years, how the hell would you handle that?

"Time is different for us. However, you're right. It is a long time and the world has changed so much. There are so many of you now, and the technology you have – passports, border control, CCTV everywhere, ID cards – it's not as easy as it was back in the good old days." Marcus looked up at the dirty stained ceiling, dreamy eyed for a moment as he reminisced. "Moving about can be quite challenging and dangerous. I quite like watching films though, to pass the time and keep me up to date with things. Thinking about it, I do watch lot of films." He said as this statement was a shock to himself now he was thinking about it.

William frowned, thinking this last comment seemed rather out of place, like listening to an old relative talking of their school days, then just changing subject without warning, but he let Marcus continue without interrupting.

"When I was born, the world was smaller, yes, but in another way much, much larger. You could walk for weeks without seeing anyone, yet some parts were not even discovered – the Americas, darkest Africa, the far north. Communication could take weeks, ships sailed off, returning many years later. It was a different world and we could walk amongst you at ease. When we first got with the Persians, the leaders could foretell we wouldn't be able to live and stay as we had been living forever.

Although we are more powerful than you, the sheer number of you would beat us. Numbers always mattered. As we fed on you, we feared we would be wiped out, made extinct from the world, so, after thousands of years of ruling over humans in small amounts, our elders decided to deal and work with you, a beneficial trade-off for both parties.

"Religion was different back then too. The old gods were more diverse than that stupid Christianity that came along later. Drinking blood and human sacrifice was carried out all over the known world, so us drinking human blood wasn't such a deal-breaker back then. In exchange for safety, privacy and food, we in turn inspired their minds. We helped the Persians with medicine, maths and an understanding of the nature that surrounded them – a big help in the desert.

"Later, with the Greeks, we inspired them with philosophy and waterwheels. These things helped them and were things that their civilizations needed to grow, we tried to stay away from conflict, they were so war like, things maybe have been different if Alexander had stayed alive longer than he had, but with his death a power vacuum ensured they just carried on fighting each other.

"We had helped the Persians win battles using illusions, telekinesis, altering the weather. When we were together in numbers, we were strong. Their empire grew, but so did their borders and, naturally, their enemies. To combat this, seeing what we were capable of, they sent us to the edges of the empire, hoping our magic and inspiration would help their forces.

"What we didn't know, though, was that the fewer of us there were together, the harder it was to use our powers. Before the empire, we had always been together in groups, large numbers, spread over a relatively small area, so at first we didn't oppose the idea, but the power of the many outweighed the power of the few. Things started going wrong. A few of us were killed in battle, which was not acceptable. The elders of the main three tribes then agreed that the Persians' time would soon be over. We needed to find new partnerships, ones that would continue to work with us but not split us up: cue the Greeks, for a much shorter time than we expected before moving on to the Romans."

William digested all of what Marcus had just said. For a madman, he had his backstory sorted out, he searched his mind, was this a book, or a film, he had mentioned he watched a lot of movies, nothing sprang to his mind. I mean, Jesus, it went back thousands of years and he seemed to be telling it as if he believed it, but then again, someone insane would, wouldn't they, they must all believe their own madness otherwise they wouldn't be mad.

"So how come you are here then, in America, in Vegas, of all places?" William asked.

"Sin city. Why wouldn't I be? A nice supply of rent boys and hookers to use for food, lots of people coming and going to help me remain unseen. Plus, when I need money –

which I don't need a lot, but we all have clothes to buy and bills to pay – I simply pop down to one of the many casinos – not on the strip, the out-of-town ones – play a little roulette where I can use telekinesis to, let's say, make sure I get a run of numbers. Not too much to draw attention to me, but enough to see me alright, if you know what I mean. Then there's Texas Hold 'Em, where a little mind-reading pays dividends. So, with a source of blood, a befuddlement spell to ensure they don't remember me or why their arm is a little sore. I always take care not to kill anyone, don't need a missing person's report, then, mixed with a bit of lady luck at the tables, this town easily keeps me going on both fronts."

Marcus was actually enjoying himself; he couldn't remember the last time he was able to be so open about his life with anyone – the fact that it was a serial killer he was opening up to now slightly amused him. He looked at Liam – no issue there yet, and if needed he could drink him dry, resulting in peak power to deal with William.

"So, you can't die?" came the next question for William.

"I sure can – fire, salt-water – we can get injured, but we can recover from most things, given enough time. As I said, time is different for us; we deal in decades, not weeks like you. As you have a gun pointed at me, yes, bullets will do the trick too." Marcus almost immediately regretted his honesty, giving William advice, and he cursed himself for relaxing too much.

"Okay, let's run with this. You were born in ancient

Greece in the time of Alexander the Great?" William began, whilst thinking to himself that when people regressed they always did so to an important event or were indeed a famous person from history themselves. No one was ever a maid or peasant dying of the pox or some other horrible illness. "Please, go on. What happened next? You built the pyramids or something?"

"For your information, the Pyramids were built 1500 years before I was born. I am not sure if we were involved or not. Most likely we were. Anyway, time moved on, Greece moved on, and therefore so did we, into the Roman era."

Chapter Seven

76 AD – Pompeii

Raylon walked down the darkened street as he returned from the Senate with an angry stomp in his gait. He was accompanied by at least ten Roman guards. He was not happy, not happy at all. He had informed the Senate of his people's concern: something bad was going to happen and they were at risk – not just his people, but everyone. Dismissed by the Senate as the fighting was far away up north from Pompeii, the Romans couldn't see a threat from any enemies.

The Romans had been good partners up until now; seeing the benefits for both parties, they had all thrived. The Greeks had been a temporary measure, a learning curve for the Majiksis to review where they were and what they could achieve with these so-called civilisations. Mankind was the same no matter where you went, tribal and war like, always looking at each other's lands, or who was ruling, looking to exploit, enslave or steal whatever they could, play power games. When the

Majiksis had exposed themselves to the Persian's they had been a bit naïve, they had told too many truths; they were learning about themselves as much as being learnt about by their new partners; they didn't hold back thinking that would impress the humans, it did. It still went wrong though. It was a different plan with the Greeks, after "capture" the Greeks knew they were special, just not how special, battle tactics were hidden away in favour of inspiration, philosophy and arts, they were kept far from the battle fields, in large numbers in safe cities and places of learning, their power influencing the next generation of scholars. For them it was a peaceful time although war was never far away. As time passed and the Greeks were beaten by the Romans, the Majiksis transitioned to the Romans, they had watched and adapted to how the humans interacted with each other, seen their ways and were now happy to become more involved again. The Romans were special, determined, they wanted it all, if they teamed up with them they could see a bright future, they would jointly rule the entire world, the Romans the enforcers with the Majiksis the puppet masters, this what was destined, the world was theirs the elders thought.

    The Majiksis had lost their name and were simply known as the "others" although their over-all identity was a close-kept secret. Only nobility, high-ranking officials and generals knew of their existence. Sure, some common folk were wary, rumours and myths spread around the empire, but in general they lived in secret, in a few large groups around the known world, keeping away from the city of Rome itself. Pompeii was the largest settlement with over one hundred people, next was Selcuk, then Jerusalem. They had inspired and helped first the Greeks then the Romans, the latter benefiting from the full force of their powers, not only in battle, but also in developing technology, and this had helped the Roman Empire dominate the known world. They even helped the arts. It had gone very well for both parties just how it was predicted it would. This, however, was the first proper disagreement they had encountered.

Raylon entered the large villa, leaving the guards behind the solid wooden door, and approached the other elders in the darkened hall seated in the middle of the enclosure.

"Well?" asked Hershel, a raised eyebrow formed on his aged forehead. Hershel was the oldest and wisest of all the elders and was held in high regard, he had been the driving force that had led to where they were today.

"They would not listen, stating that the battles and tribes far north are the only threat. I suggest we get everyone together, all feed at once and combine our mental power to see into this threat. There is something coming, we all feel it."

It was agreed by the elders, and all the "others" were sent for – men, women and even the children. They gathered into the large villa from the surrounding buildings and out houses. The bodies of around twenty slaves and captives that had been provided for them lay lifeless on the floor, drained of their blood, the bodies would be removed later on, no time for niceties, the task in hand could not wait. Within half an hour, the "others" had eaten and now they sat, led by the old and wise Hershel, mediating and chanting, all thoughts combined to try and use one of their rarest powers: foresight. This power was incredibly hard for them to use, and they needed not only for many of them to be in attendance, but for everyone to do the same thing at the same time and concentrate, sing the ancient hymn and help cast the spell. It wasn't a given that it would work. In their history, there had only been two incidents in the past to draw upon as reference. They sat quietly, all focusing and trying to identify this threat. The chanting and praying started but the danger was closer than they imagined, a spectra hanging over them, a low rumbling began to echo around the room, then the entire villa, was this part of the process? No one knew, confused, they continued the spell in hope as unease started to spread , pray harder was the advice from the elders, it was all in vain, as Vesuvius erupted.

Chapter Eight

2019 AD – Las Vegas

"That was the start of the end, really," Marcus said.

"The end of what?"

"The Roman Empire. I was a young man by then. My family still lived together. We were in Naples when we heard the news – an entire third of us dead, wiped out in one fell swoop by mother nature. We all felt it that night, lights going out in our minds, an empty void left behind."

"You were a young man?" William huffed disbelievingly. "By your reckoning, you would be four hundred!"

"Yes, another movie error. You have in your films and books the alien or ancient races that live much longer than you humans, don't you?" Marcus said. "Yet, they are babies and teenagers the same number of years you are. Doesn't add up, does it? I was what you would call a baby for sixty years, being cared for by my mother, then a child and teenager for the next three hundred. If you live for a long time, like we do, as I said, time is different. Funny, really – we do share near enough the same gestation period of nine months, us just slightly longer at ten maybe eleven, though. I always thought that was strange."

He continued ignoring the sneering look on William's face. "Pompeii really hurt us – over one hundred souls dead. We do not recreate like you rats, only twenty-three of us had been born in my lifetime, so something had to be done. The elders set in motion a plan for the next three hundred years. After Persia, we learnt that safety was in our numbers, and we stuck to that for the next half century. However, we saw we needed to split up for a while. Make some space for ourselves as we reviewed the new world in which we lived. The population everywhere was increasing, cities were popping up in all the lands and that was always a risk to us. We needed time and a safe space to think and assess all situations. What was our future? Where did we fit into this changing world?

"It was agreed that, in groups of no more than twenty, some smaller, we would slowly leave our Roman masters. I call them masters because that is what they were becoming. No longer did we feel they were a true partner. We were gods to them in the early days, but the new religion was changing the Romans and, in fact, the whole of mankind. Over the next hundred years or so, we spread out, all of us had firstly left the East, so we decided to head north to the new lands, a few went as far away as modern-day Scandinavia, although most of us, the bigger families settled in France and Britain as well as Spain. Others did go east, as far as Cambodia and Thailand I think, or the Khmer region, as it was to become, but most to Northern Europe."

William checked his watch, plenty of time really but he wasn't so sure now where this was all heading to, never mind the travelling roman vampires, maybe this bloke was just a joke, playing for time, perhaps he should get the hell out of there, abort this mission, in fact should he continue in his vengeful course at all, had he been lucky so far? Keeping an eye on Marcus as he continued with his tale he stood up and slowly moved across the room to the window, he slightly pulled the curtain to one side checking the street, could he see a silhouette in that car down the street, was he, or had he been followed? No, surely not, he would have noticed if he had been followed, most likely a punter looking for some action in this part of town. He moved back to his chair by now only half listening to the storyteller.

Marcus momentarily stopped talking, waited for William to relax, after a nod of acceptance he then began talking again.

"The Romans suffered with the gradual loss of us to help them. To our kind, moving and leaving them was quick, but to the Romans it was so slow, they didn't realise at first. When they did, they firstly sent their army far and wide looking for us, to bring us back. This left gaps in their defence, which were exploited by all the people and tribes they had previously conquered, who rose up against them, perhaps with a little of our help along the way." Marcus smiled deviously at this point, as if thinking back. "Secondly, the internal arguments and power struggles that the Senate and Emperors had to deal with in the aftermath of losing us, their most valuable asset, meant they went from ruling the world to collapse." He laughed.

William had been listening intently now, he had taken history at university, so he recognised the reasons given for the fall of the Roman Empire. However, he thought, if I know that, so could this guy – a quick look at Google and then make up a bit of bullshit to embellish it. To be honest, though, he was enjoying this alternative romp through history, although feeling anxious about being stuck in the room, sub-consciously he looked over his shoulder to see if there was a back way out of the chalet if needed. As he turned his head back towards Marcus he nodded towards Liam, and William saw the container was now full of blood.

"Do you mind?" Marcus asked, gesturing as if to have a drink.

William saw this as an opportunity to see the vampire in action. "Go ahead," he said, using the gun to point.

Marcus got up and walked across the room. He disconnected the container, then disassembled the homemade draining kit, before turning, pouring the blood into his glass and saying, "Cheers."

Marcus drank until the very last drop of blood. Was he just a weirdo? As William watched, perplexed, he felt it was all very odd. Did he look healthier after the drink than when William had first entered the room? Was William's imagination getting the better of him? Was what he was being told just made up rubbish, was history a lie? The Greeks, the fall of the Roman Empire, all built on lies? Or was it how Marcus was saying it, was it simply that his story was a lie?

"How has all of this been kept secret? I mean, the Romans kept records, history, archaeology and all that. How have you managed to stay hidden for thousands of years?" He wanted to catch the storyteller out. He thought he could do this in two ways, one by picking a hole in his tale, or he could shoot him, see if he healed like he claimed he could do, this action would also serve to reassert who was in charge here, he had started to feel uneasy with this man, he made a plan and prepared to spring it.

"We were and still are the world's best kept secret. The Romans did a great job, as did the royal families of Europe, later on." As Marcus made his way back to his seat, he was suddenly caught unaware by the rush of activity, William man-handled him from behind forcing his hand onto the small table provided in the room, before he could comprehend what was going on William had pushed a cushion onto his hand and shot the gun off, blasting a hole straight through his left hand, the cushion only slightly muffling the gunshot, it totally caught Marcus off guard, he hadn't expected that at all. William pushed him back to his seat, he backed away to his own chair the gun focussed on Marcus's forehead all the time, grinning like a fool.

Marcus was not happy, he was now in pain plus he was angry he had been sucker punched, he had got too carried away telling his life story and had got caught off guard, it was too risky to try anything, the noise might have alerted someone, so he decided to let it lie and not to react.

William watched him, trying to fathom out what was going on in Marcus's mind, he felt better now he had shown he meant business. After a short time with both men realising no one was breaking the door down he asked Marcus to continue, the cushion was still soaking up the blood, it would be telling if the hand just decided to heal itself as he went along he thought.

"The Romans did indeed keep records, but we made sure they were buried before we left. Neither they nor we wanted our secret pact in the public domain. If the world knew of us, our scriptures and spells, if we were out there, everyone would either want us or want to kill us, and, as I said, we can't do volume. If the Mongol Empire had us as partners, well, with the numbers they had, then, the world would now be all Mongol. Only one race has ever ruled the world: the Romans. The British came a close second, but never quite managed it. If they had kept the colonies, then who knows? Times have changed. No one nation will ever rule the world again, with or without us. Well, it would have to be without us in reality, as we are so few now."

Marcus suddenly looked sad. He paused for a minute before continuing. "I haven't felt another presence for over fifty years, and that was when I was on a train. They could have been outside as I whizzed past, for all I know." Recalling this combined with his aching hand made him angry, he had under estimated this man, he started to think of a way to get out of this situation, best to play along for now.

"What about America, or Russia? They are superpowers, aren't they? Or even China?"

"Those times have gone. Look at it this way, you have these super villains in movies, or an alien race, hell-bent on taking over the world, taking over the internet, reading everyone's emails. I mean, by Zeus, can you imagine that? How mind-numbingly boring would that be?

"Anyway, I digress. Let's say you rule the world. You will still live in a house, castle, mansion, whatever, so you need someone to build it. You need someone to mine or make the stone or cement. You will need to eat; the population will need to eat. You need lorries to move the stuff, the lorries need fuel, so, err, okay, builders better carry on doing what they do, plus the cooks. Oh, so you would also need the farmers, and ships to get the supplies here, ship builders. You see, it's endless."

"I never thought of it like that" William replied, he may have a point he thought, he was feeling more relaxed now he felt in charge, he felt a little bad now for shooting the man.

"The world works. If you take over everything, you are

in charge, but 99% of the world still needs to continue as it does. It's not like it was with the Romans and English. For all their evils, they helped the world move on – perhaps too much, particularly for my people and some other tribes. It's the same for countries, or super-powers, as you called them. You all need each other now."

Liam stirred softly and William watched Marcus after sheepishly looking for approval, move across the room and gently touch his head. Almost immediately, he went back into a trance. It was impressive to watch, but William was still erring on the side of believing that Marcus was a history-buff hypnotist with a taste for blood rather that a three-thousand-year-old vampire, his injured hand was telling him that much, as Marcus held it like any human would, having a hole in it.

William checked his watch, keeping the gun and one eye on Marcus as he made his way back to the sofa. He had been here near on an hour. This was longer than he usually hung around, but then again, he had usually shot dead two people by now. This was just a strange conversation in a rented chalet, not a crime scene.

"Okay, so your 'people' split up and went their separate ways. Where did you go?" William asked.

"We managed to still be a family for a while, as the Dark Ages came. The Empire had fallen. So much for 'diversity is strength.' That's popular now, isn't it, with your leaders? Well, perhaps they should have asked the Romans what they thought about that."

"Anyway, we, my little group, went north to France as the world became more unstable. The Goths started it, but there was huge migration from all the Germanic people, with the Islamic tribes in North Africa forming a new caliphate. Mankind overall stalled. Without our influence, inventions and arts stuttered, people looked to new religions and new gods for inspiration. We kept ourselves safe, in general, where we had settled, our blue eyes not so much a beacon to identify us in Northern Europe, although I did hear the few of us that went south were killed, making our numbers in the world even smaller. Africa I was told was not for us.

"Not a lot changed for us for a while, or the world through the Dark Ages, as your historians called them, that was until one of our elders – the one with maybe the biggest flock in France at the time – decided he had grown tired of the lowly life we had made for ourselves. Things like having to hunt for our own food. I mean, we hadn't had to do that for over a thousand years. Anyway, he decided to expose us to a rising order of knights and make a deal for our future and the future of Europe. It was a total risk, but the risk paid off."

Adam had located the rental car that had been identified still in the parking lot and pulled up along the road a short distance away, the boys in blue had come good, this was indeed the car he was looking for.

This was a really seedy part of town, any manner of things could be going on in there, he now had to figure out which chalet his suspect was in. He checked his watch, not too bad, it had taken him just over an hour to get here, he weighed up his options and decided it was best to sit in his car and wait for a while just watching the comings and goings to see if he saw anything at all suspicious, then try and work out what to do next, no need to call for back up just yet.

He wound down the window, just an inch, fresh air was a godsend as he tried to think, just what was it about Chicago that wasn't sitting right, it was really bugging him now, he thought back to his recent notes, his research, he checked his old contacts for anyone he still knew over in the Illinois office.

Chapter Nine

1177 AD – Jerusalem

A huge smile had spread across Godfrey's face as he laid down to sleep that night, not that what had forced him to smile, the cause of his happiness would be chronicled the way the battle had really played out would be ever told. After all, this was the Templars' secret. It was theirs to keep forever, sworn to the order since that day seventy years ago when Godfrey's own father, Philip, had met with these mysterious monks and made a deal, deal that would shower untold rewards on their order.

The history books would tell of King Baldwin, the teenager whose body was ravished with leprosy, standing with the relic of the true cross itself, in front of the assembled troops, God willing them to smash this wretched Muslim horde and drive them from the Holy Land once and for all. How the brave five hundred had routed Saladin's twenty-six-thousand-strong army, the biggest victory ever for the Templars. Yes, that was how it would be told and, to be honest, much of that was true.

The Knights had taken on the huge opposing army and routed them, they would have captured Saladin himself, if he hadn't so unceremoniously run away, but the darker truth was known, and would only be known, to a few, the special few, one of whom was Godfrey De Glanville.

The group had approached the Templars in France around 1118 when they themselves were a young order. At that time, they were a charity founded to help safe passage to the Holy Land for pilgrims. The trail was awash with bandits and highwaymen who would rob and slaughter these people without a second thought. The group proposed a deal in which they would help the Templars in exchange for protection and reward. Godfrey's father had told him of the display that was given that night, of their powers, and how, and if the knights took Jerusalem back, the new people could do even more for the knights. When Godfrey followed his father with he himself being sworn into the order in the most secret of initiations, his eyes, mind and entire life were opened up to the real world and how it had been secretly formed until now.

Over the next few years, the Templars, with their new allies, created the largest economic infrastructure with innovative financial techniques the world had ever known. It seemed there was no stopping them as they also built over one thousand commanderies and fortifications from where they could control the local areas – the most that Christendom had ever seen. Under the instruction of their new partners, the knights built a huge headquarters on Temple Mount in Jerusalem and began digging downwards. Much speculation abounded about what they were digging for. Hidden under the pretence of digging for holy relics from Christ's era, they were actually looking for the Roman records of the group's history that had been buried there after the fall of the Empire. This helped the monks in all their tasks and cemented the Templars importance on the world.

The battle itself consisted of five hundred knights, two thousand infantry and assorted followers and, the most important element, thirty-five monk sages, as the Majiksis or the "others" were now known, standing together, well sort of, they had left their allies alone, protected safely at the back, guarded by a trusted handful of experienced knights, they huddled together in silence as they were all concentrating, the chanting, they dutifully followed the lead monk.

They firstly used their power to inspire the Christian army, installing a no-fear spell, focusing on a simple piece of wood they had, they made the followers believe this was part of the one true cross on which Jesus had been crucified. Then they befuddled the men tasked with Saladin's baggage train, sending them away from the army towards a river that the sages had drenched in fresh rainwater, making it overflow, the surrounding area becoming incredibly muddy, hindering any crossing. These three interferences, although very draining for all involved, ensured that, when the Templars attacked Saladin's army, it would be in total disarray, poorly prepared, and some soldiers were even without their weapons, as they were not near the baggage train.

The Templars had routed and slaughtered the Muslims, inflicting Saladin's greatest defeat upon him, Godfrey was already thinking on how to tell his tale to the scribes, he wanted to make sure he was to be in the history books, the other advantage of the "others" was their part had to remain secret, that left it nice and open to get your own version written down how you wanted, as the saying goes "History is written by the winners."

Chapter Ten

2019 AD – Las Vegas

"So, you were there, in that battle?" William asked, he had spotted a trend that somehow Marcus was never actually at these events, he had been told by his family, or members of his tribe what had occurred, handy that, he thought.

"Me? No, not that one. I was in England by then, no, all these stories were handed down generation to generation, retold over campfires. We could have been onto a good thing with the Templars, but they fell for mankind's own deadly sin of jealously. Why can't people just get on, share, work together? The power the Templars had was a focal point for the other orders of the day, as well as the kings of Europe, particularly the King of France Phillip, the fourth I think, anyway which ever king it was, he had his view on the Pope and the power of the Vatican. This in-fighting led to the re-emergence of the enemy and, in ten years or so, the Templars had lost it all. They struggled on for another hundred years, but they never reached those heights again. We, well we had become a commodity, the play making, politics and wars that followed were now all about us. Those kingdoms that had more of us had more chance against those who didn't. If you had us on your side, you had the power.

"Instead of being exclusively with the Knights Templar, we were shipped about to be with the kings now, the royal families of Europe. We went along with it, we were still being looked after and the humans really understood our value, we were from three main tribes with smaller family units as well, there were at least twenty of us in Spain, thirty-ish in France and forty to fifty in England, with perhaps another sixty spread around the known world as far east as modern-day Thailand. England was where I was now. We liked it there, as it was an island, and many of us had found our way there on our own.

We were soon joined up, as the French knights settled there and brought more of us with them. My father had passed away from old age and my mother was getting old too. We lived in Warwick Castle most of the time, helping inspire mankind. Every now and again we would be let out, usually if we were needed for battle purposes. We were aware that with this fighting we were coming up against our own kind, but we knew it was a way of consolidating us together as the time and battles passed, It was an okay life, we were looked after and well fed, but it was nothing like the old days with the Persians, Greeks and Romans. During the Dark Ages, we had lived lonely lives away from each other. Yes, we fed, but we felt empty, the overall feeling whenever we managed to meet up with other tribes or family members was that we missed inspiring these lesser beings. Compared to what we had accomplished with the Romans, our northern cousins helping the Vikings become expert ship builders and navigate the seas was nothing. Do you know how silk is made?" Marcus asked.

"Err . . . It's a worm, isn't it?" William answered, a little taken aback at the sudden change of subject.

"Yes. They eat mulberry bushes. To protect themselves, the worm wraps itself in silk. This protected it for thousands of years from its predators, until mankind discovered it.

"So, although there are now more silkworms than ever on the planet, all are farmed, and most are killed – boiled alive before they even have a chance to spread their delicate wings – to make silk shirts, skirts and underwear. The ones that are kept back are for making more babies to be killed before they reach adulthood. That's how we were back then: the power we had to protect ourselves became our ultimate downfall once we had exposed ourselves to mankind. We were slowly becoming prisoners again. Yes, we lived in a nice castle or monastery, fed regularly like the worms and were looked after, but we – who, let me remind you, were once gods – were now, for want of a better word, slaves to humans.

"You humans just kept fighting, breeding and

multiplying. When I was born, there was not even a million of you in the world, even if you counted the undiscovered parts. By now, we were up to five hundred million people. Today, it's eight billion. It's crazy. Where do you think it will stop?" he said.

"What followed were petty battles here and there, well everywhere really, it was endless, a siege, a raid, all under the guise of something else, but really to flush us out, take us from our current masters and force us to join their cause, be it the French, English, Dutch, whoever. We were losing our independence as the French and English came out on top, who, ironically, were near enough the same people, in our view. This went on, back and forth, back and forth, for over a hundred years. Us being used to swing the tide, but no side ever winning outright. We were a great asset, if you could use us properly then the world was yours for the taking, but as the Persians had found out to their peril, we couldn't do everything or be everywhere."

Chapter Eleven

1415 AD – France

Sir Thomas Erpingham looked across the battlefield straining his eyes to see the amassed French army. His spies had informed him that the French Knights numbered some thirty thousand and, from his own view it looked frighteningly accurate. Other numbers had been as high as thirty-six thousand, some as low as twelve thousand. No way was it as low as twelve thousand; he made a mental note to deal with that spy later. Whichever it was, thirty or thirty-six thousand massively outnumbered King Henry's six thousand men.

Not so long-ago they had tried to escape back to England via Calais but had been cut off. Tired, hungry and disease riddled, the remaining army was here at Agincourt in Northern France. He looked at his men, English and mainly Welsh longbow men, brave loyal soldiers that had been with him in France for quite a few months now. They looked downhearted as they faced the odds, but Thomas knew of the ace up their sleeve. He glanced across the misty field at the tents, finally focusing on the one that contained their answer. The red tent was now part of every English battlefield's army, but the men knew nothing of what was really inside. Henry had managed to acquire sixteen sages for this campaign, by all accounts a huge amount. To keep them a secret from his men, he had just brought women and made out they were his personal whores, for his use only. The men were not happy, but there were other "camp followers" available.

Thomas, however, was happy with the overall battle plan and layout. After all, it had beenv tried and tested under King Henry's command, they had done this over a hundred times. It was the odds they faced that bothered him. They had expected a surprise attack the previous night but thank the Lord that didn't happen. He had sent a messenger to Henry explaining that his men were ready and in place between the two sets of trees, spikes in the ground, facing the French army. He then patiently waited whilst keeping a keen eye on the occupants of the red tent.

Silvia led the group of sages. She was over one thousand, six hundred years old and had seen many battles – some were lost, but most won. Her thoughts drifted to Montgisard and the Templars; she had been there and was glad she'd played a part in that battle. After fleeing the deserts of Persia, she never really had time for the Arabs preferring the company of the Europeans. The land where they now called home was far prettier in her view, and they seemed to have more fun, like with the Romans. Anyway, back to the task in hand, she and her fellow sages held hands and focused. Following her lead, they swayed and chanted, the needed spell forming, Yes, that should do it and swing the tide. The old ones are the best ones. No need to reinvent the wheel. The wheel: it was her grandfather that had inspired that one, he had told her. Feeling confident, she smiled. Today would go down in the annals of history, she knew and could feel it.

Thomas readied his men as the French signalled their attack. The message had come back that Henry was confident, and everything was in place, he looked at the growing French army in front of him, a quick glance back to where he could see the just the top of the red tent, he hoped, no he needed their friends to be on their game today, this wasn't going to be easy.

The noise from the French horses increased in volume as the mass charged, as they came within range the longbow men began firing, the hum of arrows almost silent against the thunder of hooves, the ground however had become incredibly muddy. Yes, the French sort of expected it a bit, it was quite natural and normal, but this was unreal. The horses now under intense fire simply couldn't move. The only ones that could were the panicking animals that had been injured. It was a disaster. Completely stuck in the mud, they were at the mercy of the longbow men, as man after man dropped to the ground. Those not hit had to dismount in the chaos and try to make their way forward to the awaiting men-at-arms protecting the archers. With sixty pounds of armour, visors down for protection, dodging rampant injured horses whilst walking around and over fallen comrades in this unbelievable mud, the French knights were doomed.

Thomas' men just fired and fired until they literally ran out of arrows. They were still heavily outnumbered, so, even though it was a massacre, the French were so close, the English had been shooting at point-blank range. The earth beneath their feet as solid as rock, arrows spent, Thomas remained calm as he ordered his men to reach for their hatchets, mallets and swords and start to smash, cut and crush the enemy before them. The French, seeing how close they were, a valent last grasp for victory sent in their second and last wave of men. However, this only added to the chaos as they caused the mud to become even more clay-like and restricted the movement of the men at the front, not allowing them to be able to move back and flank the English.

After three hours of heavy, bloody fighting, the battle finally was over. The French blood mingled in the countryside mud; Henry and the English had triumphed so impressively against the massive odds.

Thomas was organising the counting of the dead, ordering his men to clean up and reorganise the camp when the order came through. In an unusual move, the King ordered the prisoners to be executed. This was not normal procedure and

Thomas was angry at this change of tactic, it wasn't right, what if they had lost or didn't win the next battle, should he expect the same courtesy, there were rules for these encounters especially for high ranking knights . As he went to confront Henry, he saw at least fifteen men in chains being taken to the red tent. Aware of their fate he decided to blank that from his mind. He knew that, without that mud, he could be the one in chains – or, worse, dead – and he was certain where that overly sodden earth had come from.

As the history books would read it was a good day to be an Englishman.

Chapter Twelve

2019 AD – Las Vegas

"Right, let me get this straight, one more time, bear with me if you think I am being a little slow......here goes. You and your lot, your kind, have been alongside mankind since God knows when, feeding off us, drinking our blood across time, until now. No one has a bloody clue you exist apart from the Romans, the Templars and all the Kings and Queens of Europe? Come on! That long, that many people and no one let the secret out, come on you expect me to believe that, someone would give the game away. I mean, the Romans kept records and certainly the hundred-year war was documented." Although William was enjoying the overall story, he was starting to think it was all bullshit, plus more importantly, he was becoming conscious of the time he had been in the room, pointing his gun at a lying weirdo – aware he was holding a gun that could be linked to other recent murders, - perhaps this man was a potential killer that he had just met by chance and could still get the better of him.

Marcus was still sticking to his line that he was an age-old human like, blood drinking, super beast, it was starting to grate on William. He looked at the hand he had shot and was happy and somewhat relived as he noticed that it hadn't magically healed just yet.

"Great lengths were taken to keep us secret," Marcus continued getting equally frustrated at the repeated line of questioning, maybe it wasn't such a good idea sharing, he wasn't used to spending so much time interacting with anyone, he lived a solitary life most of the time.

"As I said, we were the world's best commodity. Ironically, gunpowder from the orient, was not being used for guns, oil only used for lamps, and whaling was not wildly exploited yet. We were the best thing a nation could have, and we were just on the verge now of the Golden Age of discovery. What do you think would have happened to those daring expeditions from Europe if we hadn't been involved? When they landed in the Americas, that whole continent was still in the Bronze Age. That's what your world would still have been without us. Mankind was everywhere, but we were only from Persia and we were now firmly part of Europe's success." Words just dropped out of his mouth as if he had forgotten about William and Liam. He was on a roll. "Of course, there were rumours, stories and certain people that wanted shot of us altogether, but we were useful to the leaders and innovative in our hiding techniques."

"Like what?" William asked.

"Well, you've heard of werewolves, witches, warlocks. Vampires, as you know them?"

"Yes."

"Well, we made them up, with the help of the people in charge all to throw you, the common folk, off the trail. Made normal people think they had seen this or experienced that, keep them scared and controllable but within the parameters that were agreed. Witches were a great smokescreen to what we were up to and the peasants loved a good burning at the stake. Okay, a couple of us might have found our fate that way, but we were cleverer than you. We, along with the Church and Royals, hid behind folklore and superstition. Some knew but kept it to themselves in fear of being killed, like Joan was. Others thought they actually were us and ruled their little part of Europe drinking the peasants dry and butchering them in offerings to some unknown ancient god, whilst we lived in a castle in the English countryside or were bound for the west on a ship."

For the first time since he had entered the room, William was concerned. Either Marcus was mad, totally mad, or even worse he was telling the truth. His hand didn't seem to be bothering him at all now. Common sense made William believe that Marcus was insane. After all, he was drinking a rent boy's blood an hour ago, but this last speech – well, more like a rant – made the hairs on William's neck stand on end. Either way, he came to realise that he was in a room with a total loon, and definitely a dangerous man. There was no way he could tell how this was going to play out and, even with the gun in his hand, he wasn't so sure now whether he was in control. His mind returned to the room and the history lesson Marcus was still giving, he was feeling like he wanted to know the entire story, how Marcus had got to be here today, was he a vampire, was he even hypnotising William with his story telling, should he be concerned that the other man was getting the upper hand in this more than strange situation he had found himself in.

"The Portuguese had ventured further south than the Spanish to Brazil – that was an error on Spain's part, let me tell you. Whilst the English, Dutch and French were staking claims to North America, with us alongside them, the locals didn't stand a chance and, once settled, the Dutch were quickly dismissed by the more powerful English. More powerful because . . . ?" Marcus raised his eyebrows at William.

"Err, because of your kind?" he replied, now totally feeling like he was back in a lecture in college.

"That's right, because of, as you say, my kind. England had taken even more of us over the past century of war and now there must have been eighty of us under their control. That was more than the French, Spanish, Portuguese and the Dutch had altogether. I remember hearing at the time that Japan was so scared they went into self-exile from the rest of the world, only to emerge hundreds of years later having fallen way behind. No influence from us, you see," he added smugly.

"Although our overall numbers had dwindled since Pompeii, we were beginning to feel settled. The English used us well. They had us at their universities, inspiring the students, making sure that any new inventions were perfect before putting them to use, not jumping the gun on anything, taking their time. We were making sure that, when away from England's shores, they had the advantage over the natives, not just weapons like the musket, but the spinning wheel, scissors, bottled beer, navigation tools, the knitting machine. All of these gave England stability at home and enabled them, from that base, to explore, conquer and colonise. We were the driving force behind it and, although we now knew our place, we were enjoying life again.

"Not since the Romans had we felt so useful. Sure, the French were always a thorn in the side of the English, pitting us against our own kindred, competing to explore the world, sometimes winning, mostly losing, but the world was being formed to how it really is now, one you would recognise on a map or globe."

"So, what went wrong?" William asked.

Chapter Thirteen

1759 AD – North America

They had sailed up a river that no one thought navigable and set up camp. They had now been on this mission here for three months, three hot summer months, with many an illness-riddled soldier. All the men here knew that the window of opportunity was closing as autumn and then winter came closer. They hoped that the officers knew this as well. Jon himself didn't fancy being in an army tent again, in the harsh cold bitter winters that were so common in this new land.

Jon and his unit had been lucky a month ago, when they had attacked the French from a newly formed beach head. The bombardment although consistent had not been enough, and they soon came under heavy fire from all sides. If it hadn't been for a massive thunderstorm, the English troops would not have been able to pull back in time and would now be dead or captured. They had had a lucky escape.

The English this time for once outnumbered the

opposition, but the French had the height and fortifications on their side. The many attempts at drawing the well dug in enemy out had so far failed.

The two sides had sat opposite each other for months, with just some small skirmishes to show for all the efforts. Jon knew things were about to change, though, as a new ship had arrived some five days earlier. Jon, a seasoned soldier, had seen this happen before: a stalemate in some far-off corner of the Empire, a few failed attacks, and then the reinforcements arrive, but not of the battalion type. These reinforcements were but a small number of people – a small, but special group. The men, himself included, were told that they were from the military academy back in England, trained in battlefield tactics. Jon didn't believe any of this. Half of the newly arrived team seemed to be female for a start, the way the cloaks covered their bodies a dead giveaway, and he knew there were no women in the military, let alone at university, so that theory was ridiculous. He knew two things: one, it was a lie; but, two, things certainly seemed to go their way once this new group arrived.

"We are doing what?" Jon asked, upon being given the new orders, what he had heard was making him nervous, it wasn't a good plan, any soldier could tell you that, it stank of desperation.

"Shush, keep your voice down," came the reply, as the boat he was in sailed upriver.

Jon and thirty other soldiers huddled down low in the

boat as it was halted at the French sentry point. Captain Donald McDonald as Scottish as his name implied spoke to the guard in perfect French and with a near-perfect accent. Jon had been unaware that the captain could speak such impeccable French. He listened to the conversation but could not understand a word of what was being said, and he didn't care. It worked well as they sailed past.

Once landed, the men set about rigging the ropes to hoist the cannons up the cliff face. This seemed crazy, thought Jon. Who on earth ordered this, this was a mess, certainly a last throw of the dice? He was sure they would all die here or go home failures. He looked to the men around him: all of them had similar expressions on their faces, betraying their thoughts. What were they expected to do? Not only climb a cliff face but take cannons up there as well! Orders were orders, though. The men took the strain and held the ropes tight as they half-heartedly obeyed. Much to his, and it seemed everyone else's surprise, the cannons felt like they were made of feathers. The expressions on everyone's face immediately changed to joy and determination. It took all their constraint not to cheer loudly and give their position away. It had taken less than twenty minutes to haul the cannons up the cliff face. The men were now feeling buoyant as they ascended the cliffs themselves. They made light work of the hundred-and-seventy-five-foot climb, even the loose shale beneath their feet seemed to act as a ladder rather than a hindrance.

By dawn, Jon and the rest of the army were on the heights overlooking the city. The men were in high spirits, for their leaders and commanders had pulled off a brilliant tactic and outsmarted the enemy. Victory was certain to be theirs; Jon was sure as he loaded his musket. He paused for a moment, remembering the last ship to arrive with its mysterious cargo. Who were they? Did they really help General Wolfe come up with this crazy plan to scale the cliffs? What military school would have thought of that? He didn't get much more time to think about it, as the French were now only sixty yards away. Jon, along with four thousand other English troops, took aim and pulled the trigger.

In less than an hour, the French were beaten and broken, not only in Quebec, but in North America. General Wolfe lost his own life that day, but he died knowing that this battle had effectively ended France's interference and stake in this part of the world, he would go down in history the way he wanted to, serving his country.

Chapter Fourteen

2019 AD – Las Vegas

"A few things, really," Marcus said in reply to William's question of what had gone wrong. "As I mentioned, we don't reproduce anything like you do. Since I was born, only a handful of other young had followed. I don't know why. Perhaps because we had left our homeland. But, whatever it was, it was definitely slowing up. The older ones were dying of . . . well, just old age. No one, not even us live forever.

"We had lost people in the wars, especially once cannon fire became commonplace. In the old days, a city would be ransacked, and the troops would find us, or we would help them find us using a mild mind control. As warfare changed, you flattened cities and sank ships. We too were vulnerable to these things; we wish we had never shown you the power of gunpowder. The Dutch had lost all of us by now, along with the Spanish and Portuguese. We had either died, been killed or escaped, so there may have been a few of us still alive, dotted around South America, I don't know. The French took heavy losses or had us stolen from them by the British, leaving only a handful. Not knowing what to do, they hid us in the mountains, awaiting a new plan, safe, but practically useless.

"It was only the British who had us in a big enough number to be of any use. Content with superior battle tactics and weapons and seeing other countries' losses of us, their greatest asset in war, we were mainly kept back in England for safety, where we forged the industrial revolution alongside them. Stupid, really, looking back, as from our point of view this caused a population boom for mankind. We still hadn't learnt anything, the more of you there were, the harder it was for us to manipulate you and equally for you to keep us secret. Keeping us secret kept us safe. The more people who saw 'things,' the harder it was for us to wipe out memories. Sure, if it was one or two people it was easy – a baby could do it. But twenty, thirty? No way. Plus, science in some countries was leaving religion behind. In other nations blood suckers would not be tolerated by the God-fearing general public, it was troubling times all round, we were becoming lost as people, no direction and all the time being reduced in number.

"It wasn't all plain sailing for England. The American War of Independence and the upcoming French Revolution would keep the Empire busy, but these wars were different. Huge numbers of men were now involved, massive armies with modern weapons on both sides. This wasn't a handful of natives to subdue or slaughter, this was Europeans versus Europeans – well, Americans. But, let's face it, they were Europeans in all but name – and it was having to be done without our help, guidance and powers. England desperately didn't want to lose the colony, so I, along with my sister Mia, my mother and a few others were sent there in a last gasp attempt to keep North America British." Marcus's eyes looked as if he could see out of the window to the distance.

He is putting on one hell of a performance, William thought. Now he's coming to the Boston tea party. Can't wait for his involvement in Gettysburg, or perhaps he assassinates Abraham Lincoln. He smirked. I need to check on his injured hand in a bit, see if it has magically healed, maybe the truth will come out.

Time was passing Adam thought, as he checked his phone for any missed calls. Sitting in the car playing the waiting game he had managed to wipe three chalets off his hit list as people had come and gone, it was nice to see two occupants were just holiday makers, an out of towner type family in one, and a group of lively looking lads off to "break Vegas" on the tables he bet, good luck to them he thought, also, he had put a call in for any recent deaths in and around the Great Lakes area; that was the call he was waiting for.

Just as he was looking at his phone it shone into light.

"Hello, Adam speaking."

"Hi, Adam, Farid here, sorry for the delay, listen, been checking the scene, no homicides like anything you have however you will get a kick out of this" came the reply.

"Go on."

"We have a fatal home invasion, real messy affair, over in Wicker Park, you know the area?. Very nice part of Chicago I tell you, put it this way we never get a place like that on the federal wage, all property retailers, lawyers, doctors, you know the type of place. Anyway, shit happens, no arrests or even suspects, things being like they are here, double homicide, the victim was a teacher and his mother a lawyer, a certain man named Gary Smythe-Barlett."

Adam sat in silence, that name sounded so familiar, why did he know it? He wracked his brain trying to remember how or where he knew it from.

Farid continued filling in the details. "He was the main suspect at the Mach Ville massacre, you remember about fifteen or so years ago. The rich kid, main suspect, whose mother was that hot shot lawyer, she mixed in the right circles, knew the right people and the case was quickly thrown out, not enough evidence or something. You remember the case, don't you, that poor kid man, ugh?" he shuddered as he recalled the injury report.

Adam certainly did remember it. He was over the moon as he hung up from Farid, a smile spread from ear to ear as he thought of his enhanced reputation for solving this case. He was so on fire with this one, chalk it up to the "Edge." His main suspect was not only back in the country but someone who was complicit in the destruction of his family and his church had been murdered, in suspicious circumstances, a random home invasion, as if! It was all too convenient, Billy had to be the killer. Now he just needed to work out which chalet he was in and what was he doing in there that was taking so long? That was the only bit that wasn't sitting right, he was at a crossroads, he didn't want anyone else to be killed, but he didn't want to do anything to jeopardise the case, act too soon, he weighed up his options.

Chapter Fifteen

2019 AD Chicago

Gary shifted nervously in his seat as he sat in the back of the cab. He was on his way to visit his mum, he hated having to go and see her but when she called he went, that was how it worked, had done for the last fifteen years since she had literally bailed him out.

He wondered what was so urgent that she needed to actually see him, she usually just wired money into his account each month to cover his rent amongst other things. His job of teaching nowhere near covered his bills. He should have been thankful really, other people wouldn't have been so lucky, he knew that, but what he also knew was that it was her and her ways that had made him be at the march that fateful day. If she wasn't so stuck up, so "The American Dream" type, he wouldn't have rebelled, wouldn't have needed to show her another darker side to this wonderful country that she loved so much. She didn't know what is was like for the poor people, the ones who lived not only in poverty but fear, constant fear of police brutality as they went about their daily business.

After getting poor grades in college, she had helped find him this job through a friend of a friend. In the job he was able to teach the younger generation what the real world was like, how they could help it, become activists and change the system. He hoped that if Victoria could see him now she would be proud, but in reality she probably wouldn't be. After Mach Ville, she and all the others had deserted the cause. To some people it was just a hobby, something to burn off in your youth at college before joining the rat race and becoming the one thing you were fighting against. Victoria was one of them, she wasn't around anymore, she was happily married, selling boats to millionaires in her spare time.

As the cab pulled up to the electric gates of the house they failed to open, so the driver pulled over and Gary paid with the app on his phone. He got out and walked around to the side gate to let himself in. His thoughts returned to why she had called him here, she sounded off on the phone, perhaps she was dying, cancer or something. Oh no, it better not be a new man, although she had looked after herself he just couldn't picture it, not at her age. How shit would that be, it better not affect his allowance if it was.

He knocked on the front door, then entered without waiting for his mum to answer it. He shouted a casual "Hello" that echoed around the large hallway, there was no answer.

"Where was she? First she summons me here, then doesn't open the gate and now she's not even here to meet me." He searched the downstairs before making his way upstairs calling out hello as he went from room to room, no reply to his greeting.

William was waiting upstairs with Gary's mother, Anthea. He had her gagged and handcuffed her to a chair in the bedroom, amusingly to William using her own handcuffs. He had found them in her bedside cabinet, the kinky bitch. He had been looking for some hosiery to use, but these were much better, plus it made him happy knowing he would be ridding the world of another deviant.

William had been on American soil for just a month, he had been busy doing research. The Mach Ville case was well known and had been well documented, it had been all over the news. He didn't know where to find Gary, but it didn't take him long to learn enough about the lawyers involved in getting him off to formulate his plan. He found out through news articles that one of the lawyers was Gary's mum, so he targeted her. After spending two weeks of watching and following her, he found out her routine and where she lived. In his view she was as guilty as the man who had thrown the Molotov in the first place, blood was on her hands, it was double bonus she was his mum, two birds with one stone.

He had taken his chance as she made her way to her car in the multi-story she always used when she was out for lunch with the ladies. As she pressed the fob to unlock it, he smashed her in the face with a tin of beans he had picked up earlier, immediately telling her he meant business as her nose bloodied. He forced her into the car and holding a knife pressed against her belly told her to drive to her house, the sharp point of the knife ever so slightly piercing her expensive silk blouse. She was petrified, she was trying to work out who this man was - all the felons she had ever been involved in getting locked up ran through her mind - she didn't dare think about what he wanted or what he was going to do to her.

Once at her house he told her to call her son and get him to come over, with the knife still on her she did as she was told. After she had made the call, he pushed her up the stairs and into her bedroom, still holding onto her as he searched the drawers and found the handcuffs, he used to handcuff her to a chair in the room. She was thankful that rape wasn't implied or acted out, that was a start, but what did he want? He wasn't ransacking the house, didn't ask for her purse, he just wanted her son there, what had he done this time? Did he owe money to gangsters again, drug debts? Where had she gone wrong in bringing him up? She couldn't put it all down to his father's genes could she? He was a dick of a man, but Gary, she had always feared he would be the end of her, now the prophecy was playing out.

Just like playing out a scene in the movies, she saw her son pass her room and look in the door. As so many doomed people on screen she found herself shouting into her scarf that she had been gagged with and jumping the chair up and down in a last desperate attempt to warn him not to enter the room.

Unlike so many characters on the silver screen, instead of running towards his bound mother to help her out in her predicament, he did just the opposite, he did what everyone in those films should do, he turned and ran away leaving Anthea stranded, tied to the chair. That little bastard didn't even try and save his mother, alright it was what she was trying to convey to him, but she never expected him to actually do it, that little weasel.

William, who had been standing just out of sight to the left of the door could tell by Anthea's face what had happened. He had come too far now to mess it up, he chased after Gary, he had the knife in one hand and the tin in the other, he really needed to get a gun were his thoughts as he threw the tin with all his might, luckily landing square on the back of his targets head. It knocked him off his pace as he staggered forward, this small lapse enabling William to make up the yards on him, he lunged with the big kitchen knife catching Gary right in the kidneys. Gary fell forward, tumbling down the hard, wooden staircase, blood spraying up the expensive flowered wallpaper as he crashed and bumped downwards.

He landed in a heap at the bottom, his side leaking blood, his nose smashed from the fall and generally battered all over. William ran down the stairs and pounced on him, in a flurry of stabs to his body he killed the man who had hurt him so badly all those years ago, years of pent up rage finally escaping.

William sat there, next to the body, this wasn't how he had planned it, how he had envisioned it over the years. In his mind he would play with him, make him suffer, do to him what he had done himself, an eye for an eye the bible said, he had even toyed with the idea of just cutting his privates off. No way to go back now, this was his destiny to act out all his thoughts of revenge that had been building for his entire life, starting with the mother, no witnesses and to be fair she was just as bad as her son, using her power to keep a guilty man free.

She could hear him returning, it had turned so quiet after the screaming, which now seemed like hours ago. She had given up struggling, it was of no use anyway. She wasn't sure how she felt about her only son dying, after all he hadn't tried to save her, his own mother, he had turned and run, he had always been useless she thought. No time to dwell on that, she had a plan, her only chance, she thought.

He entered the room, covered in blood, she gulped. She had imagined what was going on downstairs, resided in the fact Gary was now dead, but nothing could prepare you for the sight of your son's blood, so red and so much drenching his murderer.

He moved towards her, although no luck with the handcuffs she had manged to dislodge the gag enough for her words to be audible, she tried to make eye contact; isn't that what they say, show them you are human.

"Listen, please" she gulped, "I will do anything,

please.....I'll suck you off anything, oral, you don't have to even free me, I'll do it like this, please" she begged. She thought if she didn't fight back, if she pleased him he might keep her alive.

He stopped; he shook his head as a tight-lipped smile became just visible on his face. What a degenerate he thought.

Great, she thought, it might be working. She watched him place the knife down on the bedside table.

He took off his blood-stained hoodie, then his T shirt to reveal a sad, horrendously scared torso, he turned away from her as he unbuckled his belt and let his trousers fall to the floor, apart from his English mum and the nurses no woman had ever seen his never regions, this felt right though.

Anthea prepared herself. Come on, I can do this, I can leave this part out of the police report she was thinking. It would be worth the risk, he might leave me alone after, or it could buy me some valuable time, someone might come looking for me, save me just in the nick of time.

As he turned around she swallowed hard, it was then she saw the true extent of his injuries, for just that one second she felt sorry for him, then she realised her plan was out of the window.

"This is what your son did to me...... the same piece of shit, you got off" William said. The venom in his voice all too clear, she knew right then and there he was going to kill her.

William stood in front of her and waited, watching the look of shock and realisation spread across her face. He let her take in the sight of his damaged body, this was more like it, make her suffer, like he had. Realising she was now ungagged and about to scream the house down, he grabbed his knife and plunged it into her skull.

As he sat on the plane he was feeling pleased with himself, he had come through, he hadn't bottled it, he had actually enjoyed it, it may not have been textbook, but he had done it and got away with it. He decided to distance himself from the area, he was looking forward to carrying on his mission somewhere warmer.

"Ladies and Gentlemen, please fasten your seatbelts as we are about to land, the local time is now 21.00, please alter your watches by two hours, thank you."

William was now in Las Vegas.

Chapter Sixteen

1781 AD – America

Not only did the British have the largest sea power the world had ever seen, they also had the assistance of the Sages to aid them: Marcus and Mia along with Ursula, their now frail, aging mother, and nine others – cousins and friends – were on board. For eighteen months now they had been at sea. Although the sea was a natural enemy of the Sages, they had been kept safe and looked after.

Perhaps it was being desert born, the dry lands of their past, or who knows what, but saltwater burnt them immediately upon contact and would completely dissolve them if they were exposed for too long. They had been helping, aiding and fighting this rebellion, as the British saw it, or a revolution, as the Americans claimed, along with the French. So far, all the sea encounters, thank the gods, had gone their way.

They were informed that they would be heading to Yorktown as the British forces there were besieged and needed reinforcing or even evacuating.

Ursula gathered her two children and the rest of the Sages together, they sat in the hull of the ship as it bobbed along the waves, "I am not long for this world," she said factually. They all knew it. At well over two thousand years old, she was one of, if not the oldest of their kind. "I feel it is time for you to move on. I see there is an opportunity arising here. Combine and use your powers not for the British, but for yourselves. There is a whole new world west of here, an untamed wilderness. White man has not even scratched its surface yet. You could be free there, make a new tribe away from the wars, go back to a simpler life."

Mia looked at Marcus and he returned the gaze; they knew she was right. They were just being moved around the Empire wherever they were needed to help the Brits, it was no life really. They would have to forget the others left in England and those elsewhere in the world and make a break for it here in the new world. Perhaps they could rule over the natives, make an army and send for more of their kind. Maybe they could rule the world like they always should have done, not bow down to these hairless chimps that just didn't stop, one thing at a time though, no need to let their imaginations get the better of them, there was still work to be done before they even reached land.

They called for the ship's captain, Julian Marksman, a man well aware of his cargo, for he had been with them for the entire trip. He was handpicked along with his elite men to take them where required, feed them and ensure they helped the Empire win against this uprising.

"We have had a vision; you need to hear this" Mia said. "The French are not all where your spies and intelligence are suggesting in Chesapeake Bay. They have a ship of our kind hidden. Not as many as us, but we can feel them, hidden in Mobjack Bay. If you take us there, we can convince them to join us. Our numbers will increase, and we can join together to quickly end this war."

Captain Marksman thought over the suggestion. It wasn't like him to ignore orders – that's why he had been given command of this ship and the important cargo - she was so persuasive though. He was told that the forces were blockaded in and needed urgent help, but something was telling him this made more sense, this was a better plan, he knew the area involved, they might be onto something. He could be a hero of the war, the saviour of the colony. Going against his training and orders, he turned the ship's direction and set sail to Mobjack Bay, ordering his men to be on the lookout for the French vessel.

Part one complete, the Sages thought. He was a strong-minded man, the Captain, but he was no match for twelve of them, all concentrating on the same thought.

The ship sailed into the bay as a dense fog seemed to come from nowhere. Marksman had no option but to let Ursula, Mia, Marcus and three others up on deck to help them navigate. He knew it was a bit risky, letting this many out unchained, but so was running aground.

As soon as they knew they were close enough to make it safely to land, they implemented part two of the plan. Ursula nodded at her two children, a sad smile on her lips, she then nodded to the other three. "It is now time. Good luck." She turned back towards the Captain and his men, walking to the edge of the boat on the opposite side, she climbed the rigging and, before they realised what was going on, threw herself overboard. Marksman panicked; he knew what saltwater did to them. She wouldn't last three minutes. Mia and the others threw extra confusion on the men on deck as Marcus ran down the stairs to free the remaining Sages from their cells.

When he returned, he saw Mia and the rest of them were standing still, staring and concentrating all their thoughts on confusing and befuddling the sailors, who, in turn, were running around like headless chickens, Marksman himself barking out totally contradicting orders one after another. They saw their chance and all eleven jumped into a lifeboat. They paddled quickly away. Some, exhausted from the episode, collapsed. As they did so, the fog they had generated began to lift and the confused shouting on deck subsided. They knew it was a race against time now, some were already worn out, they had used a lot of power already, the confusion, the fog as well as the actual rowing, the spray from the waves burning little freckles into their soft, vulnerable skin.

Marcus saw the damage of the shot before he heard it, as

Alexia's - one of the other fleeing sages and a friend of his - head exploded, she dropped dead into the boat. As they had moved away from the ship, their spells had stopped, either no longer in reach of their power expelled, and the sailors under the leadership of Marksman, had quickly got their act together. Marcus looked to the shoreline – maybe another ten good strokes would do it. Gunfire was ringing around them now, luckily the aim not as true as the first shot, they bobbed about on the open waves which crashed against the boat as they got closer to the shore.

Marcus was sure that it was shallow enough now not to cripple them, he couldn't risk jumping in and melting their legs off, they would soon be recaptured if that was the case, he personally had never had any contact other than a few drops of spray from the open sea, that was bad enough, he shuddered to think what actually standing In the stuff would do but they were running out of options. They all jumped out of the boat, Marcus felt a slight stinging sensation in his legs as the water worked its way through his thick trousers, which turned to intense burning when he reached the shore. He helped Mia out of the water. She was lying there, exhausted from the exertion. He did not have time to save the other three, who were also wiped out with exhaustion, still in the boat. Marcus, Mia and five of the fit enough Sages made a run for it into the trees, scattering in different directions, each taking their own chances against the gunfire. Marcus and Mia stayed together; they were family, after all.

Marksman and his men made the shore not far behind them. He completed a quick headcount. One had drowned on the ship, the old one, one or two were shot and three were still in the boat. Should he pursue the seven who had made a run for it or take the three? Either way, it wasn't good; the ones that had run were obviously fitter than the ones left behind. In the darkness of the trees, his men spread out. He didn't fancy their chances; who knew what tricks the Sages would play. He ordered his troops to take the unlucky three back to the ship. They would be made to help win this war. Once won, Marksman hoped he would be allowed to track down the bastards that had got away and put them in chains for the rest of their damned lives, he hoped that's what would happen, he wasn't so sure his failure would be ignored.

Chapter Seventeen

2019 AD – Las Vegas

"My mother paid the ultimate price in sacrificing herself, not only for her children, but for her kind, allowing us to be free again after such a long period of time in what could be perceived as captivity," Marcus continued. He looked up at the ceiling thinking of his mother and the brave act that she had done, even though in truth she was so close to the end of her life. It still hurt him to this very day whenever he thought of it.

William thought, At least he was saying he was actually there this time, this is all bullshit isn't it? William was beginning to get frustrated with Marcus, but still he wanted to listen to what he had to say. He was intrigued by him and his tales.

"By now I was getting tired of all the fighting, I just wanted a simple life, maybe a human that understood what I was, let me drink from them willingly, live side by side, but all of us, my kind, your kind were just as bad as each other. I sometimes think how it could have been, there was enough to go around for everyone, still is." He stopped talking and pondered just for a moment, thinking of the modern-day cartels, the violent drug wars, anyone could see there were enough drugs to go around for everybody, it was all about the power and who held it, it always had been, and it always would be. He then moved back to the past, starting his story again, picking up where he had left off.

"As you know, the British lost the war and, with the problems with the French, they didn't have either the manpower or the inclination to try to reclaim America for a while. Whilst Mia and I went out west past Kansas into the unknown, England, once France had been defeated, eventually went east and south to India and Africa. How much my brothers and sisters were involved, I didn't and don't know. As I said, France was down to virtually none of us, England maybe less than thirty by now. I guess a few of us were rogue across the world – Norway, Sweden, or even living under their noses in England and France. As a species we were near on extinct as far I know," Marcus said.

"So, you're telling me that all this went on, all these wars, inventions and historic events, all involving you – well, your people – and no one had a clue, only the top Kings and Generals? I mean, come on, it can't be true. Surely someone would spill the beans," William said. He was aware he had gone over this before, asking the same thing, but he was trying to wind up Marcus, make him slip up, contradict himself. A little niggling doubt kept asking "What if it was real?" Could Marcus, if he had special powers help heal his damaged body? Would that be possible? If it was, could it help him move forward with his life and change the direction he was going in? For now, he would continue to hear him out.

"I didn't say no one knew. We were a tightly kept secret, but yes, generally the population didn't know. Remember, there was no internet, news channels, phones or cameras, word of mouth and stories were always there, but it was important to keep us secret. Before films were made, there was folklore and myth, across all nations and cultures, every race on the planet has tales of blood-sucking beasts somewhere in their past– I suppose it was all based on us and what our ancestors had done before we partnered up with you. Bram Stoker wrote in, erm, around 1890, of Dracula, based on Vlad, but Vlad wasn't one of us, I told you, he was just mad.

"When film started being produced, it wasn't long before Nosferatu was made, hinting about us, but he didn't look like us, he was a monster. Film followed film, but they were based on each other and Dracula, not really on us. Any real facts about us just got distorted beyond recognition. You wouldn't watch any of them and see a link to me, would you? Mixed in with the diversion tactics we had always employed – werewolves, black magic, myths and the dark arts – we and the powers that be kept ourselves out of the focus of the general populous. I would say that the film which portrayed my kind the closest was Interview with the Vampire, as it showed our journey across time – well, the book did more than that film. Such a good film, really, but the follow-ups were awful. You strike me as a clever man, apart from what you have seen in modern film and popular culture, did you really ever believe in the supernatural? Do you even believe now?" Marcus asked.

William didn't want to answer this, time was moving on and both men felt that this scenario they had found themselves in would soon be at its end. Unbeknownst to each other, they each started thinking of their choice of end game. William had the gun and had proved he was willing to use it; Marcus, being freshly fed, had faith in his own powers. He knew his hand would be healed soon. It was becoming a Mexican standoff between the Vampire and the serial killer.

William was certain that he would not stage the room like the previous murders: Liam had to die – he was a dirty little rent boy, after all, and payback was the sole reason William was even here in the first place; Marcus, he was just unsure about – he quite liked him in a strange way, but he was unsure of him, if he dared admit it, even a little scared of him. When he was recounting "history" or his stories he seemed so intense. His eyes were focussed on something out of the room, his voice dramatic as if on stage, his arms gesturing, swiping the sword or firing the gun, William might still not actually believe him, but he was certain that Marcus believed himself and that made him dangerous. William decided to use this against Marcus. He thought, if he could get him ranting again, it might open a window of opportunity for an attack. Marcus was a witness to him breaking in and brandishing a gun that he had fired, that could bring unwanted heat, and that could spell trouble for him.

"So, that was it, then. You disappeared into the wild west and have been here now for . . . what? Where were we? Seventeen . . . err 83, so 200 plus years, in Vegas? You didn't meet the Wright brothers, did you? Or Jessie James?" William asked, knowing his words would annoy Marcus somewhat, making him think he wasn't taking his life story seriously.

It worked; Marcus looked at his assailant with his cold blue eyes, trying not to let his anger show. Who did this guy think he was? He had been more than polite with this person who had barged in, even shot him, enough was he enough. He had been busy forming his own plan, the original plan that had worked so many times before: hire a food bag, one that no one really cares about, drag them off to some shithole on the edge of town where no one wants to see anything; hypnotise, drink, wipe, befuddle and move on. He had done it a thousand times, but this time William had chosen to get involved by intruding upon him, this ending would be different.

Although it had been fun reminiscing about his past, he was now regretting that he had not befuddled William when he had first interrupted him and entered the motel room, Marcus knew he should have got himself the hell out of there straight away, that opportunity had passed now. He could be in the casino now, making some money, or at home watching a movie. He was unsure what to do, he had a few options but what was best? William still had the gun pointed at him and Marcus knew it wasn't just for show. However, full of blood, Marcus was confident he could befuddle, distract or even take over and make William put the gun in his own mouth. Although that last option would be very draining - it would make him weak, maybe too weak to escape before the noise brought attention to them - Marcus could soon feed again on either or both of them, but it all took time.

Biding his time, he decided to finish off his story whilst deciding what course of action he would take.

"Not at all, we met no one famous, witnessed no world changing inventions, for us it was a time to keep low and reassess our options, learn to live on our own, we were used to living in small groups, never just two of us, but let me tell you, you will like this one, I am sure." Marcus smiled reassuringly at William, trying not to give anything away or that he was forming his own plan of escape.

Chapter Eighteen

2019 AD – Las Vegas

"What the hell is going on in there?" Adam asked himself. He had narrowed his quarry down to one maybe two chalets. The situation was starting to get annoying. He was having concern about his initial hunch as to who the "Dickhead" killer was. He wasn't used to doubting himself and he didn't like it.

His mental image of himself collecting another medal; the large gathered crowd clapping, amazed at his detective skills; the look on his wife's face as he told her of his promotion; the royalty cheques from his memoir, which he'd written after such a glorious career . . . Well, he had to admit he was getting a tad carried away with that last one, but he had had plenty of time to think whilst waiting outside. It must be coming up to two hours now. It now looked like "the Edge" had got it wrong this time, when it looked so good just that short time ago.

There was something weird going on in there, he just knew it, but then again you could say that about ninety percent of these motel rooms. Should he just call it in, let someone else take over? Should he take a quick look himself? Should he go to the chalets have a listen at the doors, find out which chalet it was? All these questions spinning around in his head. His gut was still telling him this was his man. Perhaps the victims had overpowered him; maybe his MO was that he killed them and waited for two hours before leaving, or he waited two hours then he killed them, toying with them as the spectre of death hung in the room around them? That seemed too much of a risky path to take.

"Go big or go home," as they say in Vegas. Just as he was getting out of his car thoughts of his wife and children unexpectedly popped into his head, this was odd, he was usually so focussed on the task in hand, not in a bad way, it didn't mean he didn't love his family, on the contrary, Ellen, Daisy and Marty were his first and foremost priority, always had been no matter how he tried to pretend otherwise. They had been together for ten years now, he loved her; her spirit, the way nothing was too hard, she was a great mother as well as a fantastic businesswoman. When not being a Stepford wife you could find her working at her father's shooting range and gun shop. This was where they had met when Adam had been practising his aim whilst on holiday. The shop also kept her busy and occupied enough that it was no issue for her husband to be away from home on his various assignments, she was the true driving force behind his success. She manged to be what was seen as a traditional wife, bringing the kids up, keeping a tidy house, maintaining her looks and figure, at the same time, successfully running the family business, whilst her husband cleared the world of bad men. She had pretty much taken over the range and shop when her dad became semi-retired, standing on her own two feet, not needing her man to look after her. Funnily enough in this world that made her unpopular, especially with her sisters and the soccer mum crowd, it sometimes seemed the people in her world were just as bad in their own ways as the people in his world, at least you knew where you stood with the scumbags he dealt with, less back stabbing, more stabbing to death, considering that, he guessed that maybe she had it the best way after all.

It was a work thing for Adam though, he needed a clear train of thought, no distractions when he was on the job - distractions could get you killed in this line of work. That's where he was body and mind, to have the ability to almost totally forget about his other life, he wondered why this time his mind was travelling elsewhere, he hoped it wasn't a bad omen. No time to dwell on that, focus he told himself, it was show time.

He decided to walk along the front of the building, perhaps take a little glance through the window, if possible. No guts, no glory. He would never forgive himself if he was right and walked away, he made his mind up. He got out of his car and tentatively made his way towards the chalets.

"Adam." A hushed, almost whispered voice called from

behind him. He turned to see a heavily pregnant woman a few yards away. She was about five foot six, slight of frame, pretty face with bright blue eyes and dressed in a trouser suit.

"Sorry, ma'am, but do I know you?" he asked as he instinctively put his hand on his revolver holster.

"It's me, Special Agent Denise Cole. We worked together on the first murder, up in Boulder. I've had a couple of weeks off with this," she said, nodding towards her big belly. "It's given me time to think and do some of my own digging. I guess we have both come to the same conclusion. Is our man in there?" she nodded towards the chalets.

Adam was confused. He tried to straighten his puzzled thoughts. The first murder had been in Boulder, but he didn't recall this agent at all, or did he? Somewhere in the back of his mind, she seemed familiar, plus she looked like an agent, but before he could question anything further, she said, "I spoke to Tony, he thought you could do with some back-up. Sorry I'm late, but I'm glad I got here in time. Is the perp in there?" She nodded in the direction of the chalet.

"Err, yeah, I think so, it's either this one or the one over there" Adam replied, typical Tony covering his back. "I was just gonna . . . gonna . . . erm, take a look." Right now he felt unsure as to what he was planning to do.

"Cool. You take the front and I'll go around the back," Denise said confidently, as she ushered him along the path to the first chalet.

"Okay, good plan," Adam said gathering his thoughts. What was wrong with him today, need to concentrate, shaking his head to clear his mind he then made his way towards the front door. Denise disappeared swiftly out of sight towards the back.

Oh, Denise Cole, he recalled now, never one to forget a pretty face. Yeah, yeah, that's it. I was with her at the academy, I'm sure. She's a good agent, he was happier now of the assistance , not being sure what he was up against and feeling a tad off his usual game, he was thankful of the back-up.

Chapter Nineteen

1872 – Atlantic Ocean

Mia looked angry, but Marcus could see the lines of concentration etched on her forehead as she searched for an idea, a plan to once more get them to freedom.

They had had a good run, after escaping Captain Marksman and his crew. They had made their way across the war-torn States to the relative calm of the west – not quite the wild west yet, of the cowboy's era, but a massive natural area with rivers, trees, mountains and deserts, all sorts of different climates and landscapes, along with it had to be said, mostly hostile Indians. Not the most populated part of the world, but that suited Marcus and Mia to a T, the terrain reminding Mia of their homeland, far, far away.

They had split from the others that had made it safely to shore, a difference of opinion on where they should go, they had thought New York was the best option, blend into the darkness of the huge city; the siblings, well they had other ideas, following their late mother's idea, it was just the two of them. They knew the British would not be happy with their betrayal and would hunt them down, so they were relieved on how the war played out in the end, they could relax away from the army for a while, they hoped. Away from civilisation, they were unaware of the Napoleonic wars and the exploration of the rest of the world. The Victorian period passing them by as they made their way around what is now known as Arizona and New Mexico, keeping away from white settlers, preferring just to feed on lone Indians or the odd runaway slave.

This continued for nearly seventy years – a short time to Marcus, but a long time for man. America was now playing on the big stage, having thrown off the shackles of the Empire, and some who had fled the revolution in France sought refuge in the New World. There were riches to be had. One of these men was Claude De Mark. He was from a long line of high-ranking officers in the French Army, high enough up to know of the Sages' existence. He knew that during the war a few of the dwindling source of them that the British had captured had fled into the wild west and he figured that they could be of use – a new use, away from the arts, war and inventions. After some research he had seen back in Paris, he believed that they could be used to harness their powers for mining, to find gold or diamonds. With the promise of fortunes to be made, he set off with his team of men, mercenaries, hunters and killers, hard men, to track down these people who could make them all rich, especially him.

That's how Marcus and Mia had once again found themselves captured. Marcus had warned his sister it was a folly to go to Denver, the place was too big, however Mia wanted to go shopping for new clothes of all things, it paid off to keep up with trends and she had been wearing the same things for literally years. Their luck ran out and after a brief altercation, a trap set, they were easily caught and put into chains. Mankind was always learning, and these were a complex set of chains, no simple mechanism that could be bent or moved to enable them to free themselves. Plus, they were kept hungry, only being fed when their captors wanted something in return. This was the worst they had ever been treated in all their years by any captor, but what choice did they have?

Claude was right: his bet paid off. These beings could sense gold, be it in a river or underground, and he and his team of loyal men became incredibly rich very quickly. In fact, he soon found out, too quickly if that's possible. Becoming one of the richest men in California over night didn't go unnoticed by the Government and the President Zachary Taylor, he himself, being a high-ranking Major General, suspected something was afoot. He dispatched his best men to find out what was going on, hoping his suspicions were correct that some Sages were on American soil, these magical beings that had helped other countries take over the world.

This could be America's time, with their huge natural

resources and the Europeans on the wane. This could be the final piece of the puzzle, America's Empire. What he didn't know was that the Sages were down in their numbers, only about thirty known in the whole world. They would never be able to help countries rule like before; mankind in America would have to do it alone.

Claude had taken to gambling in a big way, he loved poker and was now able to bet big, this was to be his downfall. After losing a fixed game he called his men to join him to extract revenge on his losses and subsequent beat down, not knowing the whole thing was a trap set up to entice his crew to the same place, bring the two sages with them. After an uneven matched gun fight Claude and his men were no more, to rub salt into the wound all of his assets were seized along with Mia and Marcus.

Captured by the mercenaries, then freed by the government – well, freer – Marcus and Mia were moved about the country to help look for more of their kind. It was slow going and unsuccessful. They didn't want to find any others in the first place, and they knew they were a rare breed now. Not knowing what else to do and feeling despondent with their situation, the couple just settled into the life they now had, they would escape at some point, but they took the opportunity to learn what had changed in this new land since they had gone AWOL. With the changes of Presidents, less focus was given to this task, and their kind was becoming extinct. It was like they were being written out of history on purpose. Their low birth rates combined with the lack of any real need meant that the end was in sight for this magical race of beings.

Having covered much of the mainland states over the years, it was now that they found themselves on this brigantine, once again on the sea, bound for Italy. American spies had informed the officials that fresh sightings of Sages had been seen in Rome. They thought they could send their team over there and steal them back to America, as rumours of war were surfacing. The USA was now where they had been striving for and was a main player, some in power thought it wouldn't hurt to cover their bets. No sightings had come from traipsing all over their own country, the government at the highest level were running out of time and patience. Maybe if they could gain a few more of these Sages they could learn from the past and how the Europeans had used their resources. Nothing else was happening at the moment so why not was the general consensus.

What no one knew was that this was that once again this was a trap. Marcus and Mia were being stolen from the Americans to be used again for mining, but in Africa this time, the Germans and Boers being behind it.

They had set sail in a merchant ship to stay inconspicuous; however, they had been betrayed.

Mia was awaken from her sleep to the sound of canon fire. The ship wasn't hit – it must have been a warning shot – but screams and shouting erupted from the decks above.

"Wake up, Marcus," she whispered trying to gain some

urgency to a now awake Marcus. He moved towards the bars of their cage, concentrating on listening.

The captain came down the stairs and approached them both. "We are being boarded," he said, fear evident in his voice, as he nervously fumbled with the keys to unlock the cage. "We need your help, or we are all doomed." He knew that he and his family, as well as his men would be for the chop, but there was no way they would kill Marcus and Mia; they were the only commodity on board – the alcohol listed on the manifest was a ruse. He hoped to use them to bargain.

They followed him up onto the deck, both trying to work out what to expect and what they could do. Fortunately, they had been recently fed, as bad weather, really rough seas had caused all sorts of issues for the captain and ship. They had helped him navigate through it. All things considered; he wasn't a bad man. He had treated them well whilst they had been in his custody. Maybe he feared for the safety of his wife and daughter, who had accompanied him on board.

Three men, dressed in civilian clothing, stood on the deck before the captain, crew, and the captain's family members, their rifles raised. Their main ship could be seen just off to the portside of the mast. They had caught the crew completely off guard whilst they had been eating. They had not been expecting any trouble here, out in the middle of the ocean.

"You know what we want," said the one in the middle, with a thick German accent, as he nodded towards Mia and

Marcus, their blues eyes giving them away. The lack of insignia showing he was of no higher rank or in charge, this told Mia they were privateers, this wasn't a government thing, this worried her.

Marcus could hear Mia speaking to him in his head; she had become very powerful, with a huge array of talents, over time, so much more so than him. Most of their kind could dabble in this or that, cast the odd spell when full, when not up against any duress, but their true strength was when they were in numbers, that's when miracles could happen, storms brewed, castle walls demolished, lakes frozen, amazing feats from the past sprang to his mind, now though, most of their kind just followed orders on what to think and what to do when required. Mia was different, one in a hundred. She was a born leader just like her mother before her. She would be the one to not only think of the plan, but the one to start the thought process and act on it in an instant. She was a rare breed, someone special.

Her voice said, "I am tired of this, one prison after another, serving a different master from one day to the next. Our kind, we are done for if we continue this lifestyle. There must be over a billion of this scum by now. How can we all survive? You need to promise me that you will try to live on, though, you have always been different to the others. Don't try to stop me doing what needs to be done. You have a part to play in this world, you just don't know it yet. Promise me you will survive, go back to America, learn more, find a new way, then find more of us. Promise me!"

The man was still talking, but Marcus hadn't heard a word of it. He thought back to his mother, who had taken her own life at sea. He knew if Mia had made her mind up there was no stopping her. It's odd, but he didn't feel the need to join her in her planned suicide, even though he was only forty years younger and was now over two thousand years old, he too felt his time was not up. He waited and watched.

Mia raised her arms and everyone on the deck froze apart from Marcus and the Captain's daughter. She then turned around; Marcus could see the strain on her face as she tried to control twenty-one people. This was a lot and it would take it out of her, even though she had just fed.

Within two turns of her body, all the humans were now harmonized – an old spell that made the victims copy you. The only thing you could do was make them willingly kill or injure themselves. Now facing the same way as Mia, copying her every move, they followed as she began walking to the edge of the boat, lined up like lemmings on the edge. A look of terror was engraved on each of their faces, they came to realise what their fate was as they gazed out at the cold sea, but they were unable to do anything to stop it. Her voice entered Marcus's head again: "What are you waiting for? Go!" it practically screamed.

Marcus scooped up the young girl and made a dash for the lifeboat. He got in and set the rope going as he looked back to Mia, the crew and the invading riflemen. All together, they jumped into the sea below. The spell enabled her to complete this, as just jumping into the sea wouldn't injure or kill the humans. However, Marcus had now lost his sister to the same cruel fate that had taken his mother all those years ago.

His boat hit the calm waves with a thud, enough so that the little girl, not expecting the thump, being caught off balance, hit her head and was knocked unconscious. That suited Marcus, wasting no time he began rowing as fast as he could, fighting the tears in his eyes, he needed to stay focussed, no time for sentiment now if he was to escape.

As he rowed away, he could hear voices coming from above him as more men from the invaders' ship had embarked. They sounded panicked. He hoped they were too busy trying to rescue their comrades to notice him in the water. As a precaution and to throw them off his scent, he summoned a small fog cloud – not massive, as he wanted to preserve all his strength for the journey ahead, but enough to make the Mary Celeste vanish from his view and therefore him from theirs.

He rowed hard into the night, heading back towards America. He was tired when the girl finally awoke. It was going to be a long route, he thought, but at least he had enough food for the journey.

Chapter Twenty

2019 AD – Las Vegas

"Well, that wraps up that mystery nicely." William said sarcastically as he grinned. He hadn't seen that one coming. The Mary Celeste! But he'd had enough now. Time for action and a close to this soap-opera tale across the ages. "So, you killed – sorry, drank – the little girl and made it back to America?" he asked.

"Yes, I had to do what I had to do," Marcus said remembering the last life he had ever taken. "There is a surprising amount of blood in people, as you can see from him. I don't need a lot to survive, but sadly I had a lot of rowing before me."

"And Mia? I get it, it's like Keyser Söze, The Usual Suspects. Mia: Missing-In-Action. I get it. You really do like your films, don't you? You know what? I've had enough of this bollocks."

Marcus shuddered as he did his best to ignore his

agitator. What was that? he thought. Did he just feel what he thought he did? It had been such a long time. He was so deep in thought, trying to work out if something new was afoot, that he took no notice of William, even as the gun unloaded a single bullet into Liam's docile head, splattering his docile brain and bits of skull all over the tacky wallpaper of the chalet.

William pointed the gun at Marcus. "Not how I usually do it, but you know you are a witness now, no hard feelings," and he shrugged his shoulders.

William expected to just pull the trigger and be done with Marcus, but for some unknown reason he hesitated, pausing long enough to doubt himself. Shit – is this Marcus, the vampire, making me hesitate? Is he in my head? Is it all true? Oh my God, I could be on the verge of the biggest find in human history. Why did I shoot the rent boy? As the panic crept in he faltered in his plan, the door was flung open.

"FBI! Freeze!" shouted the man now standing in the doorway, expertly holding a gun in both hands.

Adam had heard the gunshot just as he'd approached the door, two seconds earlier he would have been in the room. It was time to act, he kicked in the flimsy door with ease. He quickly surveyed the room as he entered taking in as much detail as he could whilst maintaining his own safety, the perp standing pointing a gun at an unknown man on the sofa, another unknown man, head wound, dead, on the chair. He was right all along: Billy was the Dickhead killer. Slightly different MO, but it had to be him. Adam did his best not to smile at his own brilliance, he would make sure he had time for that later, now he had to deal with the room.

William didn't know what to do, two seconds ago he had it all mapped out, now he was in a truck load of trouble. His gun was pointed at Marcus, who was unarmed still on the sofa. The FBI man had a gun pointed at him – he looked like he knew what he was doing with it too. There was no way he could alter his aim and shoot him without taking one himself. Plus, was he on his own? They always had a partner, didn't they? The speed at which he had kicked in the door meant he had to have been close when William shot Liam. Were they onto him? Was there a mass of officers outside? His thoughts switched to Marcus. What would he do? What was he? William knew he was a weirdo, what with the blood drinking and all, plus now he was believing his story, why couldn't he have just shot him when he had wanted to? He would be seen as a victim and would probably not be sent to jail, not with a murderer in the room. He couldn't count on Marcus to help tackle the FBI.

"Drop the gun!" Adam screamed, eyes darting from William to the unknown man.

Marcus also didn't know what to do or even what William would do. He did know that, although his hand underneath the blood-stained cushion was healing, guns could kill him, and he didn't want to go there, so he just sat and waited to see what would happen, his mind searching for anything that could help him. He could befuddle William, giving the agent the edge, but then he might have to explain too many things going forward. Surely the agent wouldn't be alone – they always worked in pairs or was the entire place surrounded? He could befuddle the agent. Without a doubt, William would try to shoot him, something he was about to do a moment ago, but would he be quick enough? He didn't think he could mind-control William, he was too strong willed and focussed, and anyway the same outcome may apply. As he sat there, he became aware of another person joining the confrontation. Must be the partner, he thought.

Thank God Denise was here for back up, Adam thought as he saw her emerge from the back room, her gun held up, pointing at the back of the gunman's head. The situation in the chalet was stranger than Adam had anticipated he thought as his eyes took in the scene he had just burst into. What the hell was really going on in here?

"Drop your weapon!" Both Adam and Denise shouted the instruction in unison, as if they had practised it.

Bollocks thought William. Death by cop entered his head, but, being only twenty-five, there was no way he was ready for that. Anyway, with his deformity, he could get an insanity plea and end up somewhere nice. No option but to give himself up. He hoped that Marcus 'the Vampire' wouldn't want to be caught either and would magic up a solution that suited them both, if that's what he really was. He had started to slowly believe the story he had been told. As he lowered his gun, he noticed the blood had stopped pumping into the cushion from his hand wound, had it healed?

"Okay, okay," Adam said, "that's how we do it, nice and—"

Bang! He took one to the chest before he could finish the sentence. William looked down at his hand, to his own gun, in confusion. What the hell had just happened?

Adam was in shock, reeling backwards when the second blast from Denise's gun hit him in the throat, ripping it apart and killing him instantly. His body hit the deck in a blood-soaked crumple.

William was now aware of what had transpired. He quickly spun around towards the other agent behind him, raising his gun to defend himself, only for her third shot to hit him square in the side of his belly. He dropped his gun and fell to the floor in pain, twisting to see a smile developing on Marcus's face. William lay there, blood pouring out of his scared body.

He remained conscious as he heard Marcus with pure joy in his voice say, "Hello Mia." A thousand thoughts entered Williams head as the truth was being revealed before him.

Mia stepped over the injured William on the floor and helped Marcus out of the sofa. William was howling in pain as he watched them embrace each other, not unlike long lost siblings.

"Wow!" said Marcus, as realised via the hug that Mia

was pregnant.

"Come on," Mia said. "We don't have much time. I will take you to the others."

"But I have so many questions; like, how did you survive? How come it took you so long to find me? Did you say 'others'?" asked Marcus, these and another hundred questions forming in his excited but confused mind.

"Move," Mia simply but confidently instructed, aware she would have plenty of time to tell all, once and if they got the hell out of there.

They both stepped over William, who by now was slipping into unconsciousness.

"What about him?" Marcus asked.

The gunshot to the face answered his question, as William's brains spread across the chalet's threadbare carpet. Aware that four loud shots had been fired they knew they needed to get the hell out of there, "William it was really nothing" Marcus said and smiled to himself as they left through the back door, hand in hand, reunited once more.

Chapter Twenty-One

1872 AD – North Atlantic

"What are they doing sir?" Dieter asked his senior officer as he viewed the ship ahead. To the naked eye, it looked like everyone on board had climbed onto of the edge of the boat.

"Shit – row quicker," Hans commanded, immediately realising what was he was seeing, he had read about these creatures and their tricks before the mission, he knew he should have sent more men in the first boat, he was annoyed at himself. "She must have them under a spell or something. All hands row quicker!" he shouted as they made their way to the ship to help their comrades.

Everyone watched as they all jumped simultaneously into the waves below. Hans and his men were about ten metres away at this point. He knew what saltwater did to these things. He wasn't concerned for his own men, nor the captives, at this point, they would be fine, just the targets. He was told there were two, but he could only see one woman who didn't look like the other crew members as she disappeared under the cold water.

Mia felt the burn as soon as she was submerged in the saltwater, burning her eyes like she had acid injected directly into her very tear ducts. The rest of her body reacted as if she had run into a furnace, the reaction was that fast. She welcomed death; it couldn't come quick enough.

She had passed out from the pain as two men swam towards her and secured the rope. Hans and two more of his men heaved her on board the small boat.

As they gazed at her smouldering broken body and melted face, Dieter vomited over the side. "Too late – she's done for sir," he stated.

Hans disagreed, partly from knowledge he had and partly because he knew the price of failure. "You will be surprised; they are very tough. It may take a while, perhaps longer than our lives, but she will live," he surmised hopefully. "Now, get the others out of the water. We will take them with us for the time being. And search the ship – I was told there were two," he further ordered.

With that, his men obeyed. After rescuing their own men and the crew of the Mary Celeste, they searched the entire ship before returning to their own vessel. By that time, Marcus was long gone.

Chapter Twenty-Two

1117 AD – Northern France

"It is time and agreed then," Shalob said with authority to the assembled crowd of elders. They had decided that they no longer wanted to hide in the shadows. Times had changed, and they must adapt to it as well.

 Babock, Shalob's young son, watched on in disbelief. He couldn't believe that his father was the one planning on making a deal with the humans after all this time. Had he forgotten how Rome had ended? How they were not the rulers of their own destiny like they once were in Persia or with the Greeks? His father had been there in Pompeii, he even voted to move on, away from their relationship with the Romans, let the stupid fools fight and kill their way into extinction. But instead they had just bred and bred. Babock was not happy as the elders planned his future.

 Babock was sure the future should be theirs; they were top of the food chain, not these killing and breeding machines.

He wasn't the only one that thought differently, though. Lots of the younger ones wanted a new life, a life they should have, one they hadn't had a chance to enjoy like the elders once had. Good times, to them, were just campfire stories, ancient history of better, happier times. Watching all the elders leave to consult their own kindred, Babock approached his father.

"You are wrong, it won't end well, there are too many now," he rambled, cursing his emotions for getting the better of him so that he couldn't put forward a structured sentence or argument.

Shalob turned to him. He looked weary. "You are too young to understand my son. You do not know. You were a baby when we left Rome. This is for the best. They have changed, evolved – even without our influence, they have evolved. We need to make an alliance with them and live the good life, no more being on the road, moving from one place to the next every time the locals work us out," he stated.

"Let me start again, me and the others," Babock replied. "We think we should be ruling these plebs. We are better than them. If you work with them, they will continue to breed and then they will enslave us again, just like Rome. You know there are too many of them. We need to ...."

"Silence!" his father interrupted, raising his hand to silence his son. "You know nothing, yet you sit here and preach. Where else do you and your young friends think you can go? The Islamic world has put a fatwa on our kind, they have been ordered to kill us on sight. The very land that we came from, we can no longer go there. We have heard nothing from the tribes that went east past the Muslim lands, even if you could get that far. No, it has been agreed: France, England, this is to be our next venture. We will rule with them, we will help them, and they will look after us. We will make them need us so badly that they can't do without us. That is the plan and that is what has been agreed by every elder, no more of your dissent and talk of nonsense, I won't hear of it again, do you hear me" an angry Shalob stated, and with that, he stood up and walked off. "I have to speak to our family now." He shouted back showing his clear annoyance at being questioned by the young hot head.

Babock left in the opposite direction. After walking three streets away, he knocked on the door of a house.

"Well, how did you get on?" asked his lover, Redel.

"It's no good. The old fools are going to expose themselves to the Knights and make a deal, just like we thought. It's the wrong thing to do, but they won't listen to us. I mean, us only being four hundred years old – what could we possibly know?" He directed his answer not only to her, but to the other thirty plus people gathered in the room.

Silence held the room for the next ten minutes as they all gathered their thoughts.

"So, what are you suggesting?" asked Matthew, one of Babock's closest friends.

"We go south, and I mean proper south – past the

Muslim lands and into the heart of Africa, or even further."

"But didn't the others die?" someone shouted from the back.

Babcock thought for a moment. "Did they? Or is that just what we were told? Told to scare us, they might be there living like gods – we don't know. But what we do know is that, if we align ourselves here with these people, it won't end well. They won't respect us, they will use us – and I, for one, will not be used, not by anyone. I – well, we may be young, but we have heart and courage; the old ones, the elders, they struggle to mate with their women, they are so weak." He looked at Redel as she unconsciously touched her bump. "I am to be a father, the youngest father ever, and you know why? Because I hunt, I do what I was born to do. I hunt, I feed, and I mate. I use my power over these weak pathetic humans. All of us can do this, it is what we were born to do. We will go south, we will take the land and become gods to these short-lived idiots."

A cheer rose from around the room as Babock finished his speech. He basked in the glory. It was his first taste of power and he liked it. It was decided he would take the younger Sages away from the flock and start a new empire, way down south, in deepest Africa. To hell with his weak accommodating father and all the other not-so-wise elders.

Mankind was changing. Even in the Dark Ages and without the influence of the Sages, they still kept increasing in numbers, expanding their culture and occupying more land.

They had new inventions, new ideology, new religions. They needed to be stopped, as Babock was certain the future belonged to him and his kind, the new breed.

Chapter Twenty-Three

2019 AD – Nevada

Mia gunned the car down the highway, feeling more secure once they left the bright lights safely behind, it was a typical Nevada night as she now relaxed and eased off the

ng, he had felt old. Perhaps the trip through history had made him think too much about it, but, before Mia had burst in, he had reviewed his life and had actually asked himself if it was time to die, to finally move on after all these years. accelerator. She was so happy to have finally found Marcus after all these years. Quite what he was doing in that chalet was beyond her, but the network information had finally come good. It would have been nice just to knock on a door and find him, instead of having to leave a bloodbath. A dead FBI agent was never good, but it was what it was, and Marcus was now safe.

Marcus was overjoyed. He thought he was alone, the only one left, the way the day had been panning out he even thought this was the end of him, it seemed odd now that thought had even entered his head. Not only was he wrong, but it was his sister that had come back for him.

Once Mia was sure they had made a clean getaway, she pulled over. Now stopped, she hugged Marcus for what seemed like an eternity. Tears welled up in her eyes, and his, and neither knew where to start, so they sat in silence just looking and smiling at each other. How long had it been? Nearly one hundred and fifty years since that fateful day on the ship.

Mia looked great. The last time he had seen her, she had been drained, defeated, old perhaps how he had looked earlier – now she seemed radiant, healthy, even youthful. She certainly didn't look her age, he thought, not like him. Back in that room, even after feedi

"Well?" Marcus eventually said.

"Firstly, I am taking us to a safe house – well, more like a compound – in North Dakota. You will meet the rest of us there. Secondly, don't ever let me jump into the sea again!" She burst into laughter, before adding, "No, seriously - don't. It was like having a boiling hot shower on sunburn, for thirty years."

"How did you survive? What happened?" he let the "rest of us" slip for the time being, he would delve into that later, he just wanted to hear her story, it was great to listen to her voice, it had been way too long, he was so happy, his big sister was back.

Mia told him how she had been rescued by the Germans

from the other ship. "I was burnt to a soggy melted crisp, if that makes sense. Then they took me to a nunnery in South Africa. Long story short, it took nearly thirty years for those nuns to heal me. They just fed me and nursed me every day until I slowly recovered." Tears formed in her eyes as she recalled the tale.

Marcus hugged her again as he too began to well up.

"How did you end up here, back in the States?"

"A friend helped set me free. Anyway, let me concentrate, will you? We are not in the clear yet – not until we get to Dakota." She restarted the car, took a quick look at the sat-nav to see how long it would take them.

"So, what now?" he asked.

"I will take you to the safe house and you can meet Babock, our leader, and, err, the father." She tapped her stomach.

Wow, yes. In all the excitement, Marcus had forgotten the fact that Mia was well and truly pregnant. She looked like she could pop any minute.

So, not only was Marcus not alone, his sister was alive, with a child on the way, and she was taking him to meet some more of them. North Dakota – wow, he had been so close and so clueless. What was wrong with him? Had he given up? he asked himself.

"Who is Babock? An elder? I don't recall him . . . No, wait – not Shalob's son? He is younger than I am! How can he be the leader?" Marcus asked, not really thinking straight, to him he still thought as them as they had been, just youngsters, forgetting that was eight hundred years ago.

"The very same, and he is not just a leader – he is a genius, he is the saviour of our people, he is shaping the future of mankind and they don't even know it," she answered, a soft smile on her lips.

Mia slowed down once she was sure they were in the clear. No need to race now they had plenty of time, and certainly no need to grab any unwanted attention from any traffic cops or cameras.

"Tell me more of our messiah, then, please. Help us pass the time." He was curious about this set up she was talking about, he hoped it was a nice place filled with sensible people, he had been on his own for so long and he was over the moon to see his sister, however over the isolation years he had learned to respect the humans and what they had achieved, he hoped to find a big version of what he had been doing, quietly living alongside in peace, no more squabbling for power, he was sure it could be done.

"You remember the time with the Templars? We went from France to England, quite a few of us, but we always wondered where some of the others had gone – the ones just slightly younger than you? Well, Babock lead them south, through the desserts and jungles of Africa and even further."

"And they made it?" Marcus asked, thinking back to how perilous that journey was thought to be, and how dangerous he was told it was.

"Yes, although some were lost on the way. Seventeen in total I think he said, including Babock, made it to Mapungubwe, modern-day Zimbabwe. His plan, instead of working with the locals, was to enslave them, and they ruled over the natives, although not quite directly. They did it through local chieftains, but not like in Europe, where we were. Babock was totally in charge.

Great, Marcus thought, this wasn't what he wanted to hear.

"They bred, fed and handed out harsh punishment to any who dared disobey them. Trade routes north were set up and, much like we did in the States, they used their powers for mining: gold; diamonds; all sorts of riches. This made them very wealthy and they lived a good life – as he would say, like gods, like how he had envisioned it. They kept away from what was going on up north and the rest of the world, just lived a wonderful, fruitful life. Perhaps the locals might disagree with that, though." Mia laughed.

"Sounds good." He lied, he decided to play along for the time being. "Well, better than we had it, anyway. Surely, though, the modern world caught up with them. It must have been at about the time we made a break for it, or soon after, that the Empires headed that way," Marcus said.

"Yes, and that's when all the planning and storing of supplies that Babock had ordered came to the fore. As I said, he is a genius. By the time the English and French came that far south, they thought we had gone from this world and they had learnt to get on without us. They had seen our numbers dwindle over the years and, after the American wars, they just sort of ignored or forgot we ever existed. Science was taking over from religion, making tales of supernatural creatures less palatable to the powers that be, and the Royal households were also losing their control."

Marcus was concerned by his sister rhetoric, it was all a bit "culty" he thought, or was he misreading her, it had been a crazy day by anyone's standards, or had he simply been ploughing his own field way too long, perhaps when they got there he would have a rethink, no need to jump to any conclusions, let's see and reassess when we get there.

"Anyway, we were ready for when they inevitably came," Mia concluded.

Chapter Twenty-Four

1887 AD – South Africa

Babock sat in his hut, awaiting the return of his friend Matthew, his most trusted lieutenant. He had sent him away on a fact-finding mission just six years ago, he felt guilty that it was always Matthew, some of the women were just as useful and competent in their work and powers, but not a lot had changed in the world and the women just couldn't get to the places of power that he required them to be. He wondered if that would ever change, although most elders in his world had been male the females were often more powerful in their abilities, he was quite content to be in charge and the leader but he had tried to share the lines of authority on talent not just sex, however if someone had to infiltrate the enemy it usually had to be a male as was the case here.

As he waited, he took stock of their fortunes since leaving what he now called the northern tribe, the followers of his father who had decided to join the Templars all those years ago.

He and twenty-five younger men and women had taken flight, heading south after they had disagreed with the elders' plan. It wasn't all plain sailing, as they lost nine souls along the way, before they finally settled here in what is now known as South Africa.

A skirmish in Tunisia that saw the deaths of the "nine" martyrs, as they became known as, it had been a real scare. As a group they had never experienced such death, it really shook the confidence of the all of them, and in truth they had all nearly given up and returned north to join the elders. They only survived by harnessing their power and causing a landslide; this not only took out half the attackers, but blocked the trail, enabling their escape. His father had warned him of the fatwa, but Babock knew they needed to get past these lands and stake their claim further south.

Although totally personally shaken by the attack Babock knew it was his chance to cement his leadership and he took the opportunity to enforce his plan, show his intent and desire for a better life for them all.

As it turned out, life was very different the further south they went. Small tribes were easy prey on the journey, until they reached Mozambique and settled there. Here, the tribes were bigger and much more accustomed to war, more like how the Europeans battled than the tribal skirmishes they had passed on their way down here, the landscape so different as well.

However, a drought seemed to be in place when Babock and his followers arrived. He smiled as he recalled what he considered a simple trick: they made the river not only flow once again, but they also froze it and walked across it before unfreezing it. Yes, it drained them of their powers, it was a risk leaving them so vulnerable, but it worked as it blew the natives away in one hit. They bowed as he walked through them to the king, who then himself bowed. They gave assistance in a battle with a neighbouring tribe and that was that – the enemy were enslaved for work and food, the tribe then grew from strength to strength, but they all knew the pale-skinned blue-eyed gods were in charge.

That was how it stayed for generation after generation for the humans, as these blue-eyed monsters ruled them. For his kind, well, this life seemed to suit them, and they saw an unprecedented rise in their own birth rate. It may have been the return to the old ways, using their powers for themselves, but no one really knew. As they were all so young, perhaps it was their youthfulness, but one thing was for sure: there were twice as many births over those six hundred years than there had been in the entire Dark Ages since they had left Rome.

Babock's flock was now eighty-four, with fifteen due as he sat there waiting.

Matthew was always chosen when Babock thought it was time to spy on world events away from their little empire. Although very young, he was brave and fearless, as well as seeming to have the ability not only to think on his feet, but to blend in effortlessly with the humans.

They had been in Africa nearly five hundred years when he was first sent on a mission north. Here at home they had honed their powers to find riches such as gold and diamonds as well as water and fertile farming land for their people, they had the slaves and tribal men dig mines where they sensed the goods were. This saved a lot of time and effort compared to how the humans did things, as no wasted work was involved on baron, unfruitful land.

As an experiment, Matthew was sent to work with this power in Mali, resulting in making its king the richest man in the world at the time, maybe ever in the history of mankind. Testing his theories, Babock instructed Matthew to help send the king on a pilgrimage to Mecca. This was a dangerous task, as Mali was back up in the Muslim lands, but Babock wanted to know for future use the effect of masses of wealth and enormous amounts of riches could have or use on the humans' lives and not just by war. As always, he was right. The king generously overpaid for all goods, or simply gave gold away to locals as he went from Mali to Mecca. This collapsed the region's economies, causing chaos for over a decade all along the route that was taken.

This was an important lesson for Babock as they stockpiled the mining extractions for future use. He made sure to remember this and add it to his master plan.

Matthew finally entered the hut. Babock was amused to

see him sporting facial hair – all part of fitting in, he assumed.

"Come in, old friend. Drink?" he offered, as a collared naked slave dutifully walked forward from the shadows of the impressive shelter.

"Don't mind if I do," Matthew replied, and he took a knife and cut into her already scarred arm.

After taking his fill, he wiped his mouth and smiled at his leader. "Well, you were right," he said: "dotted around the coast are cities controlled by Europeans – England, France, Germany."

"Germany? Who are they?"

"A young, but enthusiastic nation it had to be said. They have plans to get on the main stage, and it looks like Africa is the place to do that. They all have plans to carve up the whole continent, and that includes us, here I'm sorry to say."

Babock thought for a moment. He'd known this was coming. He had counted on it, planned for it. "What about us?" he asked.

"No."

"What do you mean, no?"

"We are not there; I found no evidence of our involvement at all. I went to England – you would not believe it – on a steam-powered ship, using coal! They have advanced so much – yes, still killing each other any chance they get – but they have come a long way," Matthew said, he sounded impressed.

"What, and without our influence? You felt, found no one?" Babock enquired. He couldn't believe it. He thought back to the time he had told his father his concerns, his thoughts that the humans were evolving on their own, but he had only half believed it himself, just trying to build an argument for his reasoning. With what he was being told now, his kind, the northern tribe, were no more, and, worse than that, even without them, mankind wasn't slowing down. "Population?" he barked, showing his anger and changing his line of questioning.

"World, about fifty million; England – well, Great Britain – near on ten million. Even with the many wars, they haven't slowed down. They now have railways and steam ships for travel, as well as a thing called the telegraph, where they can communicate over vast distances." He pointed his hand to the slave before continuing. "These tribes here don't stand a chance. They are coming from all directions, even diseases won't hold them back – they've invented medicines known as vaccines – we can't stop them." He ushered over the slave girl to refill his cup, it was good to be back home, getting fed when away had its problems, it was nice to not have to plan a meal, or forever look over your shoulder.

Babock was stunned. Yes, he'd realised they wouldn't be alone here for ever, but fifty million was beyond his wildest guess. He had plans. They were in good numbers and with good numbers came strong powers. They had plenty of resources, things the humans craved so much, but he was not prepared for the sheer volume of people that Matthew had told him existed.

"Germany, you said – same old tribes that brought down the Romans? Perhaps we have an opportunity there," he said, thinking out loud.

"Or America, that's over the Atlantic, where all the slaves were being sent. They still call the New World. The east coast is conquered, but they call the rest the wild west, a massive untamed land, virtually empty, quite a strong nation, though. Europe, they want Africa between them – not just the three I mentioned, but others as well: Italy, Belgium, they were all at it, wanting a piece of the pie. We won't be safe here much longer – maybe forty years at the most."

"Okay, get everyone to feed, then gather them all," Babock ordered, this news was very concerning, he felt they were soon to be facing their biggest threat since deciding to leave on their own, he needed to do something, act now. "Let's see if we can do what they couldn't in Pompeii." Forty years was too quick, he thought.

Chapter Twenty-Five

2019 AD – Las Vegas

Tony Lopez wiped the tears from his eyes as he sat on the kerb outside the chalet. He'd just had to get out of that room. Although a seasoned officer, having seen and attended over fifty crime scenes in his career, this one had personally hit him hard.

The tears were a combination of sorrow for his old friend and colleague, as well as the natural reaction that comes with vomiting. The scene in the room was just too much for him to take in.

Why had the "Edge" ended up in there? Who were the other two men? What was he doing here? What lead was he following? Why hadn't he called for back-up? All these questions and many more were still swirling around his mind as he clocked the sedan pull up.

He wiped his eyes to get a clearer view as an elderly, well-suited man, maybe sixty years old , along with a woman perhaps ten to fifteen years younger, equally impressively dressed, made their way past the cops at the taped boundary. He wasn't sure what agency they were from, but he was certain it wasn't FBI.

He reluctantly decided to follow them into the murder room and find out some more about the two newcomers.

As he entered the room, the man was talking to another officer. Tony thought he heard a strong, posh English accent, something he recalled from imported telly shows his father had watched years ago, Monty Python or Benny Hill. It seemed he was taking over the investigation, as his partner was slowly surveying the room.

"Come on, Tony," his boss said as he came towards him. "It's not our case anymore."

Tony was confused. They were the fucking FBI! Who the hell were these guys? Furious that his friend was dead and now he was being taken off the case, his anger got the better of him.

He pushed past his boss, who didn't offer any resistance. Perhaps he also wanted to find out more, but rather than put himself at any risk, he would let Tony do it. He grabbed at the English man.

"Who the hell are you?" he shouted, as he man-handled him.

The English guy didn't bat an eyelid, which only infuriated Tony even more. He began pushing him towards the wall, pinning him against it whilst continuing his rant, when he felt contact from behind. Before he knew it, and to his embarrassment, he was floored by the small woman. None of his comrades came to his assistance, they just stood and watched, as he was quickly put into a wrestling hold. He nearly tapped out as he was immobilised with pain.

"Thank you, Agent Abelson," the limey said, straightening out his suit jacket.

Tony's boss came over. "Okay, okay – let's all calm down," he said as he helped release Tony from the woman's grip. "Come on, let's go." He rallied the FBI team and they left.

Richard and Bina looked over the chalet. Whilst Richard made a call to their back-up team to come and clean up the room, she examined the bodies, concentrating mainly on the young rent boy and his injured arm.

Just as thoughts of her great grandfather and his dealings with the Nazis were on the verge of creeping into her thoughts, her partner, Agent Richard Marksman, interrupted her.

"We were close this time; they must be near here," he offered as he glanced at the window, imagining the roads outside.

Bina knew it as well. They were getting closer. If they acted quickly now, got the interstate cameras downloaded, they could be onto something. Finally, their targets may be within touching distance.

Justice and revenge were firmly on their agenda.

Chapter Twenty-Six

1783 AD - England

They all sat in the massive old room, it could have fitted five times more people than it currently did, but security and more importantly secrets had to be upheld, everyone knew only the chosen few could be in the know.

"So, gentlemen, we have a quandary or two that we need to discuss, to formulate a plan, it's been a long time coming, but here we are." The General paused and surveyed the room looking intensely at the six men seated in the old study, the walls covered in paintings of former leaders, military men and politicians, their grand uniforms of recent times painted so lovingly with so much more colour and variety than the faces of the old white men now seated below them.

The American war was over, the British had lost, the meddling French had done their bit, with the distance over the sea being the final straw, this time the navy and the Sages had not been enough to seal the deal.

General Martin was right, there was much to discuss, thoughts on attacking the new republic would have to put on hold for the time being, the noise from over the channel was troubling to say the least and far too close to home now.

"Okay, let's start with this chap, erm, Marksman is it?" he continued looking at his notes, "Yes, that's him, I say treason, hanging offence, any other thoughts?" he said bluntly.

Julian Marksman had made his way back to England in disgrace. He had not followed orders to help the troops in the divisive battle at York Town - things could have been so different if that garrison had been re-enforced - instead he had been hoodwinked by the damned Sages to a point of killing two and losing another seven, not good enough on any front by anyone's standards.

Brigadier Arthur Raven stayed silent, he wanted to protect his friend who he knew was a good loyal soldier. Markman's entire family served, his four brothers were on active duty even now as these men debated his fate. He wanted to defend him, point out the odds he was up against, tell them of his proud history and the brave previous fights he had been in to earn him his role of being in charge of that ship in the first place, above all he didn't want to lose his lover of the last ten years. It was a hard choice but if that knowledge came out he wouldn't be long for the world either, he may not be killed but he would be ousted, his power and living taken away from him. Against everything he stood for he decided to keep his mouth shut, he knew his lone vote would not swing the tide one iota and would just raise unwanted suspicion on why he voted that way, he vowed he would honour his friend in another way, an inside man alive could do way more damage than a loyal dead man.

"All in agreement then, Marksman is to be hanged until dead for treason to the crown, better we take out his men as well and close off the whole sorry episode" he added to the nodding heads of the jury. Just like that a death sentence was given, no trial, no jury; that's how it was to these people, as easy as tying one's shoelaces, it needed to be done and so it was with the minimum of fuss.

"Over to you then Cecil, our friends, the Sages, what are we to do with them now? Are they of any use or have they had their time?"

Cecil Waterstone wasn't a military man like all the other men, bar one, on the committee. He was a new breed of man, a dreamer, more future politics then current day, he had foreseen the American war and lobbied parliament to get ahead of the game, unfortunately his concerns had fallen on deaf ears until it was too late, now though, with hindsight, his stock had been raised and he was seen as an important part of the inner circle.

He began speaking. "France, look at what they are achieving right now, they lost most of their Sages, some ten, twenty years ago, they have but a handful, yet they are a constant thorn in our sides. We have six camps of five in the country, that is all. Let's be honest, they hate us, they try their best to undermine us, I am sad to say that the glory years are behind us now unless we learn to stand on our own two feet."

The men took in what he was saying, they all knew the history, the battles, the work that had taken place over the years as the Sages shaped the country; London, Oxford, Cambridge, Edinburgh, all of these great places had a pocket of these beings on campus. No one could argue that they hadn't inspired and enabled the learning on so many fronts, they may not have actually invented anything themselves, but these people were special, it wasn't all about battles.

"I must say, I think we leave them in the universities and the navy and army academies, leave well alone to do their thing, no more risking losing them, let them inspire the next generation for the good of the empire." Admiral Yates threw in his view.

Cecil continued, ignoring the interruption from the old man. "The general thinking is that these beings have had their time on God's green earth, they are not natural. They have served their purpose and put mankind on the right path, now it should be the righteous path, do we really think in our great cities we should have blood sucking leeches being knowingly fed by the government. It's an abomination to be honest, what if this got out?"

"It hasn't for hundreds if not thousands of years so let's not be too hasty" General Martin jumped in, trying to get the discussion back on track.

The men all sat in silence trapped in their own thoughts -

they knew the empire had done very well on the backs of these creatures, they also knew that they were hated by them and that now down to just thirty, things needed to change. A vote was coming on abolition of slavery, not a nice choice for any living being.

"One more thing before we vote" Cecil said as he broke the tense atmosphere in the room, hoping for one last chance to alter the vote. "We seem to think we wouldn't have achieved anything without their influence, but are we really that useless without them? In these isles we had no record of them before Roman times and yet we had a thriving culture and we didn't die. There is no mention of them on the Americas until us and Spain took them there, yet to the south of that continent they had built incredible empires. China, no mention, yet they invented paper, gun powder, the compass."

"Get to your point Cecil" interrupted Martin, he was beginning to tire of the man.

"The point is, do we really need these people? Have we been blinded by what they actually do? Is it time to be done with them once and for all and sail our own ship?"

The military men looked at him, they had all been in combat at some point over the years, he hadn't. He was a glorified librarian, an office mandarin, he didn't know the roar of cannon fire out in the middle of the ocean, just wood and luck saving you: the prospect of a watery grave if you didn't succeed; the smell of blood and stench of death in some hot, hell hole miles from home; someone you loved dying in your arms; or being ripped apart by cannon fire right in front of you; war was hell. He hadn't been there and seen a lost battle swung to victory by these Sages, men saved from capture or death, it was all too easy to spout nonsense when your life wasn't on the line. The men all looked at each other knowingly, they knew the way the vote was going to go, no matter how he had put the point across for killing the special ones.

"Gentlemen let's vote now, if you will. Those in favour of disposing of our...... valuable resource say yeah" a slight dig at Cecil with the word valuable emphasised.

Cecil voice was the only one to say yeah. Arthur had wanted to, but he knew the way the vote was heading, and this wasn't the time or place to expose his views. He knew where he was going after this meeting, it was going to be a slow waiting game for him.

The meeting over the men dispersed and went their separate ways. Three things had been agreed: America would have to wait; Marksman and his men were to be hanged for treason; and lastly, for now, the Sages were to stay in England on the campus's and military bases.

Arthur headed north to Leeds, he wanted to find the brothers of his beloved Julian and inform them of his plan. He hoped they would be on his side, they were good, strong, talented men, he was sure they would agree with him. These unholy creatures had had their time, it may be the generals passing the actual harsh judgement on to their brother, but he was in no doubt that it was the Sages actions that had led to Julian's death sentence.

Within two days a new society was born, its role to firstly rid England of the Sages and all their influences, next the Empire, then the rest of the world, until there were no more Sages alive. The stage was set to once and for all eliminate these soulless, unhuman, blood suckers from history. The Raven secret sect was born for just that purpose, consisting of just eight men to start with; their own government and army against them. They knew it was going to be a tough battle, but with God and righteousness on their side they would prevail, others would join them, they hoped, justice would be served.

Chapter Twenty-Seven

2019 AD – North Dakota

Mia pulled the car through the trees and down the lane that opened up to the modern compound. It was an impressive sight to see. Marcus wondered how on earth they were hiding here; it was not only massive but seemed really out of place in this landscape.

They parked the car next to an array of different vehicles clustered together, as Marcus gazed at the people working the land that surrounded the property. He counted at least twelve people out there in the cold, he could see that some were white, from this distance he couldn't see their eyes, but some were African – that meant they were not of his kind.

Mia spotted the quizzical look on his face. "We have some disciples, true believers," she explained, guessing his thoughts. "Come on, let's find Babock, he is looking forward to finally meeting you, I have built you up a fair amount" She smiled, eager for the two men she loved in her life to finally meet.

If Marcus was impressed with the outside, he was blown away by the interior. It was so smart and shiny, it reminded him of a James Bond super villain's lair or a super car's showroom. He was still looking around when a tall man approached him, his hand extended.

"Babock, I presume," Marcus said first as he took his hand in a firm shake that became a hug.

"Actually, it's now Charles." He smiled back. "Easier to fit in, you know. Anyway, welcome! And call me what you like, when here, I answer to both." Charles then turned and hugged Mia.

They went from the reception area to the back room that overlooked the land, trees and distant hills, as a maid brought over some blood-filled jugs.

Another human, Marcus spotted, as she bowed and left the room.

"So, Mia was right, I am glad to see. Her little brother was alive and kicking, and just down the road, as it turned out." Charles laughed, "perhaps now she will stop going on about you!"

"This . . . this is amazing. I can't get my mind around it – this set up, the human workers, Mia with child – it's . . . well, I don't know. Words fail me," Marcus said in honest wonderment.

"Ah, yes. Our little enclave. You haven't seen the

tunnels yet. That's where the interesting stuff goes on. The humans, well, they are devoted to us. They have seen our powers. What do we have, Mia? About thirty of them? They keep us fed nicely, do some chores, little missions for us and, in return, well, we make sure they enjoy the blood-giving with a little, shall we say, mind stimulation. No need to be crude. Such simple creatures, really," he said as he smiled.

"How do you keep this place secret?" Marcus asked, not really warming to his hosts demeaner.

"Well, our nearest neighbours are what, forty miles away, growing weed we think, so they naturally keep themselves to themselves. We have a rule that there are never fewer than fifty of us here, nearly always fully fed. If anyone comes calling, we just confuse them, cast an illusion or some trick, and they go on their way. Plus, we have a few friends in high places. It's amazing what a donation will do to the right fund raiser, in this land."

"Fifty. How many of you – us – are there altogether?"

Mia smiled as she answered. "Babock – sorry, Charles – left Africa with sixty adults and fifteen new-borns. We have others planted elsewhere around the world, working in small teams undercover, along with some humans who we have an understanding with."

Although Marcus was only one person, he was aware how rare his kind still were in the world, and even though this was the largest group he had ever known since Roman times, just adding one more member increased their power overall.

Marcus was amazed. Only yesterday, he had thought he was all alone, that his people had left this world and he wasn't to be far behind them. Now, here he was surrounded by his kind. He tried to think back to his days in England; he was sure, even at their peak, there were never fifty of their kind, this was an amazing place, no matter what he personally thought of Charles he had to admire what he had achieved.

"So, old man," Charles said, patronisingly pointing out, at his age in his brash style, that Marcus was the second oldest, after Mia, of the entire tribe, "let's show you around, whilst your sister here tells of her adventures after she tried to kill herself."

Mia smiled nervously; she wasn't sure how she felt retelling her story. It had been such a hard time, emotionally as well as physically. Looking back now it was easy to know it was the right choice, but those thirty years had been very tough. As they walked she did as requested and brought her brother up to date.

Chapter Twenty-Eight

1899 AD – South Africa

Sister Elizabeth quietly yet purposefully strode through the grounds of the nunnery. Sweat formed under her habit in the hot sun, the wetness enhanced by her nerves.

She knew that what she was about to do went against the Mother Superior's instructions, but she also knew this was the right thing to do, the Christian thing to do.

When they had first brought this maimed, burnt, near on lifeless body to the nunnery, she was under strict guidelines on how to care for her. Yes, her – as it turned out the creature was a she. It was three months before the thing before her was even recognisable as a human being as it's form slowly took shape, let alone a female.

A God-fearing woman, as Elizabeth was, she questioned at first the feeding ritual, but was told she was doing the Lord's work, so dutifully each week she fed the flask of fresh blood into the mouth of the creature, washed and cared for her.

As the months passed, the creature improved and, after ten years of daily care, she eventually managed to sit up. Most of the scarring was disappearing. Such a beautiful face it was too. High cheek bones, full lips and those lovely bright blue eyes, Elizabeth asked her name, but speech was still not achievable at that time.

She continued her duty as other nuns came and went, and Sister Elizabeth became the only carer and guardian of the invalid who she now knew as Mia, the world it seemed had tired of her and she was almost forgotten, Elizabeth would never abandon her now, she was her life's work. She thought back to when she was first given custody and how she had thought this thing should have died, should be dead, put out of its misery. It didn't seem to fit in with her teachings, what the bible had taught her, but over the years she gradually saw the situation differently.

This was a wonder. They were all God's children, weren't they? This one was special, perhaps an angel sent to save or punish mankind. Whatever she was, Elizabeth knew that God had wanted her there protecting her, feeding her and bringing her back to life.

She was forty-two when she first started looking after Mia, and now, at seventy-one, she knew her own life was short. Her last noble act would be to set Mia free and bask in heaven for the deeds she had completed for her Lord.

Her plan was to send Mia on her way to safety, before

the British came. She had heard the cannon fire every night for the past week as the war raged on. She knew it wouldn't be long before the army reached the old, crumbling down nunnery. She hoped that, as nuns, the last few that remained, they would be safe, but this was Africa. She had been here long enough, since leaving York, to know anything could happen in Africa.

Even though she was English by birth and a servant of God, she knew enough about mankind and warfare. She expected the worse, she didn't expect any special treatment for her own country- men when they inevitably came knocking, nor being a nun.

Out of breath, she unlocked the door to the cell that had been Mia's home for nearly thirty years and was pleased to see she was greeted with a smile.

"No time to talk little one," she said as she unlocked the chains that bound Mia. "We need to get you out of here. The British are coming, and I am scared what they would do to you if they found you, my sweet."

Mia stretched as the chains fell to the ground.

Elizabeth took off her headgear and offered her neck. "Do you need to feed to help you on your journey?" she asked, shaking at the reality of being bitten. Feeding time had always been from a jug previously, but she thought Mia might need the help for her journey.

Mia looked at the old nun. She had been a good comrade in the end, once Mia was aware of where she was and could talk. Her funny English accent as she had read to her each night had reminded Mia of her time in Warwick, all those years ago, it wasn't quite how she remembered the people speaking with her twang mixed with the African, but the old-world English brought back some memories.

Mia assessed how strong she felt. If she had been one hundred percent as she leapt off that boat all those years ago, she was now around ninety, she thought. Good enough for her to spare the helpful nun.

"Go north – inland, I think, would be best," the nun advised, thankful she wasn't being fed off. "The British are everywhere, but there are still lands unknown to them."

Mia nodded a thank you to her and left the cell, the fresh air and bright sunlight catching her out as she emerged into it for the first time in so many years.

As she set off north across the savannah, she thought of her brother. Where was he? Did he escape? She vowed to find him, wherever he was, no matter how long it would take, she felt he was still alive. She didn't know, she couldn't know, they may be magic, but it had its limits, she was potentially thousands of miles away, but she knew in her heart, he was still alive, like she was, most likely on his own, but alive.

Mia travelled north for three weeks, using her powers to feed or evade the troops from both sides of this latest war. Humans hadn't changed in any way whilst she had been out of the picture. By the time she crossed the river border into what she believed was Zimbabwe, she was at full health.

She didn't know why and for what reason she travelled this way, but something was calling her, drawing her in this direction. She could feel something in the air. What she didn't know was that she was about to locate a lost tribe of her people.

Chapter Twenty-Nine

1853 AD – Northampton/Portsmouth England

Hugh was looking to close the heavy iron factory gates for the day, it had been a busy month as they pulled out all the stops for the boots ordered for the latest war, he had no idea where the Crimea was but it looked to be a cold place judging by the order placed. His father would be very happy and proud that they had come through with the entire order in time. The first shipment was on its way to the docks; he had felt it odd that the man from the army had insisted that the order was made right boots first for one shipment then the left boot to follow on a different ship. He remembered questioning it in the meeting with the man, what was he called now? That was odd he couldn't even remember that, he was usually so good with names; he remembered he was a short fellow, tanned like he had just got back from India or somewhere else in the Empire, bright blue eyes. Anyway, he had been quite forceful that was how it had to be, so against his better judgement he had complied and sent the boots in two different loads, he guessed nothing could go wrong.

Gerald and his wife Betty, not their birth names, had been in England for five years now, they had been sent on a mission to review what was happening in Egypt when they had got into difficulties. This resulted in them being on a ship bound for England, it had been too dangerous to risk exposing who they were so they had blended in as much as they could until they reached dry land.

They didn't know how to get back to Africa or what they were going to do once they had docked, so they had decided to help the cause and work under cover in England to try to sabotage and disrupt anything they could. Even though they knew Babock would never know of their efforts they wanted to prove themselves as they reviewed options to get back home. The English were the enemy, so they started work behind the lines.

Betty had come up with this idea one night as she feasted on a boot and shoe worker in the Midlands; the girl had told her of a huge shipment of winter boots they were making for yet another war overseas. Betty had told Gerald about the order and they came up with a plan to firstly get the left and right boots onto different ships, then cause one ship to sink leading to whichever boot making to its destination being rendered useless, frost bite could be so cruel!

Through mind control of Mr Hugh Barrret, the factory owner, part one of the plan was already in place. They went to the docks, Gerald managed to secure the route plan from a drunken sailor, change it and get it back on the ship before anyone noticed. Betty entertained the captain where she had implanted a recurring thought to ensure he didn't question the incorrect map. They were hopeful, that following this new route, the ship would run a ground spilling its load into the unforgiving waters. They were now in a Tavern feeling pleased with themselves wishing one day they would return to Africa and inform the others of their accomplishment.

After a while they left to go to their dwellings for the night, the cold wind coming straight off the sea. As they walked against the wind Gerald hugged Betty closely whilst she pulled her heavy coat around her. He only just heard the noise above the howling wind as the pain erupted in his side, he turned to see what was happening, he was then stabbed a further three times in quick succession, he fell to the floor. Betty used her power to hurl a wooden crate, that was close by, at the attackers before realising they were hopelessly outnumbered. Stuck in the alley, blows and punches were thundered down on her, knocking her to the ground alongside her husband.

The five men carried on the attack, kicking and punching both of them as they lay on the ground, until three other men came along with a barrel on a sack barrow. They tipped the barrel forward and poured the saltwater inside onto the two fallen lovers, the water acting like acid on their skin.

They lay there broken, bruised, stabbed and burnt.

"Throw them in the jetty, that will do for them" shouted one man. He then spat at them both, "That's for my Grandad, you scum."

Edward Marksman then walked away, another good job done he thought, as the two already damaged bodies sank into the shallow dark sea water; they would never be seen again. The network was working well, men placed on the inside in the places they needed to be, combined with a great kill team, they had so far taken out twelve of the Sages over the last ten years. At this rate England would be free of them all by the turn of the century. He didn't expect to still be alive by then but hoped his sons would continue the fight.

As planned the ship had got into difficulties, hit large rocks and sunk, some say a drunk captain at fault. Only half the order of boots turned up leading to many a frost-bitten soldier, why would you send the right boots on one ship and the left on another everyone asked, it didn't make any sense!.

Chapter Thirty

1929 AD – New York

Charles sat brooding in the plush penthouse suite of the posh hotel. He knew he needed to get this one right. Things hadn't played out quite how they had foreseen, back in Africa. After Matthew's return, highlighting Europe's power, dominance and greedy plans, he had gathered every one of his tribe and tried the rare power of seeing into the future. It was a muddled, cloudy premonition, not as clear as he had hoped, but it looked like a mushroom cloud over America. Using intelligence that they had gathered about treaties, alliances and pacts, they wrongly thought that Germany was to come out on top in what would be a war like no other seen before. The humans certainly looking to outdo themselves this time.

They had rightly predicted the war, the Great War as it had been named, and had added their power and influence on what turned out to be the wrong side. He had hoped the confusion in Russia they had facilitated would have swung the tide, but the explosion they had foreseen did not happen. He had underestimated America and, once they entered the war, Germany and its allies had lost. Well, sort of. He personally felt it was like a very long armistice, a ceasefire, no actual battle had been fought on German soil, leaving the general populace confused and angry, not seeing any damaged cities, just returning broken troops wasn't war as they had come to know it, no victory parade in their capital. Charles believed this was not over and now he had set plans to ensure the next time, which he thought would be soon, it would be the end of civilisation as everyone knew it.

He felt that the biggest threat to his own people, even the world itself was the size of the human population. Whilst this kept growing – and, boy, was it growing – his kind would have to remain in the shadows. One on one, there was no question on the winner, but there was no way they could control, fool, manipulate such numbers. No, if his people were to rise above them and rule the world, they would have to wipe out mankind. Well, obviously leaving enough to control and feed off. He needed to literally bomb mankind back to the Stone Age.

To that end, he had pulled out of Africa totally now. They had put their strength behind the Boars and, although he knew they had hurt the British, he wasn't prepared for how brutally they would react against their fellow white man. Perhaps he had sent too many people with Matthew to Germany, weakening his own team's ability, but the Boars couldn't pull it off.

He had then gone against his upbringing by joining the Muslims and aiding the dervish in a last-ditch attempt to stop the onslaught. Things went well until the British used aircrafts. He hoped that it was not any of his people's doing, helping with the invention of flight. Africa's resistance was now no more, he feared for the future.

As his kind left the dark continent behind, he mused over the last forty years. He had to give it to the humans, Africa had gone from perhaps ten percent colonization, mainly around the coast, to ninety percent. It was so fast and so brutal, he needed to update their plan or face going the way of the Khoisan.

Then, out of nowhere, and nothing to do with his meddling, the Serbs killed someone important and – bang! – the whole world erupted. Like they had seen, the world war arrived, but not quite how they thought it would happen, nor – worse – how it would end. Peace never lasted with these animals.

Previously, for a while, it had, as the white man had trampled over smaller tribes and cultures, spears no match for machine guns and planes, but Charles knew they couldn't stay away from each other's throats for long. That was the human's curse and his people's relief.

Here, now, in America – what a place: huge, greedy, corrupt, violent, beautiful, powerful – he was glad he had split his forces between here and Germany. He was sure England and France had had their time at the top, they just didn't know it yet.

He was also sure the world was not done with all-out war and it was either here, with the new kids on the block, the Americans, or Germany that would prevail.

And so, here he sat, with five close friends, leaving the rest of the group in their new hideaway, far north by the Canadian border. No matter what happened, no one was invading that place for years to come. There was no reason to, not a lot there. No, if Germany won the war, which he hoped they would – well, he hoped no one would, really – but if Germany did make and drop the bomb, as foreseen, he was sure North Dakota was safe.

That could wait. He had another plan for the here and now, a plan to weaken everyone. And, when humans got weak, they fought each other better. Charles asked for updates from all his agents.

Each in turn explained: Carl was working on the steel market; Sarah, wheat and crops; Claire, houses and retail. They had all taken modern European names recently, to help blend in. They all reflected on the time they had spent over the last two years, buying, selling at such stupid prices, driving costs up, watching people reinvesting their windfall. It had always been a joyous time, working with the humans, as it had been a fun time all round in the States, with lots of partying. Charles was happier now, as he predicted the whole system was about to explode – well, "collapse" was a better word. The humans had carried on as if the stock market would just rise and rise;

everyone was buying shares in this and shares in that, investing all their money – not just savings, but borrowed money. They thought it would never end.

Happy they had played their part by investing some of the riches they had brought with them from Africa, Charles decided it was time to leave the east coast and retreat west, sit back and watch the western world crumble. Might get ten years out of this misery, he thought thinking of Mali. Buy some time. That made him smile, but the bigger plan was to invoke a second world war. When humans went through hardship, they looked to blame other humans, and that led to good old-fashioned war. That would be nice, and hopefully, this time, stoked up, mankind would finish the job. He hoped his people in Germany were inspiring the scientists over there to make this devastating bomb he had seen in his vision.

As an afterthought, he asked Claire what the square thing in the corner of his room was. A television, she explained, briefly outlining its use. Interesting, he thought, his mind already working on how this new invention could be used to his advantage.

Chapter Thirty-One

2019 AD – Denver

Richard yawned; he had been sleeping grabbing some much needed rest as Bina had driven them both north. Whilst other agencies were doing the donkey work; checking the CCTV for their targets, two non-humans, one male, the other a pregnant female, they were off to a town in the Rockies near Denver to interview a woman whose daughter was missing, claims of joining some cult or something. This was standard procedure, the boring part of the job but it had to be done. Missing people had always been around the blood suckers; this had been their original reason for being in this part of the states, until they had been diverted by the murder in Vegas. Perhaps this one would shed some light, be helpful, he doubted it though.

The day was bright and the sky clear, the sort of day you got here in the mountains at this time of year. Richard was hopeful that this meeting would come to something, too many dead ends over the years took its toll on you. He preferred the crime scenes, looking for clues, working out who did it; Was it involved with their blood sucking friends? Was it part of the big story or just a coincidence? There was no confusion back in Vegas, this was the work of the targets. They were on the run, for once he felt his side were getting the upper hand, it felt good. His family had been involved from day one; he worked his family tree out once but now couldn't remember if it was his eight times great granddad or seven times, but what he did know was that when he was hanged all those centuries ago that was when this movement had started.

His family, all military men, had been so angry at the treason charge of their brother over the loss of colonies, so betrayed by a country they had loved and put their lives on the line for, that they had vowed to wipe these sick dangerous beings from the annuals of history. Backed by some powerful people in government sharing the same view point, or wanting to break the wheel for their own personal reasons, they had set about killing any known Sage residing in England first, once that was done the secret society set its sight on the rest of the world. The more they killed the more they learned of the far-reaching tentacles these people had, they may be few in number, but they were sly, dedicated beasts. At first it had been a close-knit family thing, all about revenge but it had grown over the years to be just as powerful in its own right as the enemy they were hounding down.

Bina was a new addition to the cause, as they had

stumbled across some like-minded Israelis way back in the fifties. Bina's family, like Richard's, had a personal link, her great grandfather, being a rabbi and expert on ancient scriptures knew of the existence of these beings. Whilst trying to escape Nazi Germany to join the rest of his family, he had been caught by a group of soldiers in the same mountain area that some Sages had also been found. Trying to save his own life so he could join his family, he divulged the true identity of the Sages to his captures. His reward for this knowledge was a bullet in his head.

Bina had been brought up slightly differently than Richard. After completing her National Service, she had become a Mossad agent. As a youngster she had trained in the field of martial arts and was soon a champion black belt; she was quite formidable as well as extremely focussed. Ironically she was more of a "Marksman" than Richard was, he more of a book man, computers and lateral thinking, they worked very well together, each bringing different strengths to the team.

He checked the sat-nav, they would be at their destination in half an hour. He used the time to call the office to see if any news had come through on the suspects they were trailing. He was informed that a car had been spotted on CCTV traffic footage parked a hundred yards from where Agent Clayton's own car was, this vehicle had then been seen leaving the area around the same time as the witnesses reported hearing gun shots. From the footage it appeared that two people had entered the car, one man and one women. The car was then spotted again on the 94, not too far away from where Richard and Bina now were. This was good news, major roads around here were few and far between, but that still left a lot of hiding places in this part of the states.

They pulled up at the house and made their way to the door.

An old hippy type woman answered their knock and beckoned them inside, she looked downtrodden, beaten almost, she had seen better days. Bina noticed some tram line scars on her arms, this wasn't a good sign. They really didn't need to waste any time with a junkie, ex or not talking garbage, best to hear her out quickly and move on, get on with the real work.

"So, it's my Starlight, she missing" she started as they sat in her lounge.

Starlight, bloody hell Richard thought, typical hippy love child name here, this was going to be pointless hearing out this old hippy chick. Did she think she was getting paid? He looked across at Bina to gauge her thoughts, which seemed equally pointless as she never showed emotion of any kind, but he would bet a pound against a bucket of shit she was thinking exactly what he was at this point in time.

"Go on" he said, almost reluctantly, wishing he was elsewhere.

"Well, I know you just think I'm some old druggie; the kids name probably don't help I guess." She carried on in her overly drawn out accent and way of speaking, "I feel bad, I always encouraged the alternative lifestyle, you know, tune in, that kind of stuff, don't be a slave to the dollar, it's the type of people we are, or were. I know you clocked the scars, but I been clean now for nine months," she rubbed her arms as she said this. She had noticed the demeanour in their body language, she knew the time she had to explain wasn't long, so she hurried the story up.

"Anyways, my girl, she all I got now, but she joined this cult, and it ain't no good for her, they evil, I just know it," she looked down at her feet.

Richard was now a little intrigued, evil, that was an odd word to use, it ignited his interest. "Who is evil, the priest, the pastor, just who are we talking about?"

After a pause she starting speaking again, "Hell, they ain't no pastor or priest, they ain't even human, I know you think I'm a crazy lady, but I know what I know, they are evil."

Richard looked at Bina, she had her more than usual serious face on now. Perhaps this woman was onto something, they knew that the Sages kept slaves, it was safer than going out for food every time they needed to feed. Some people would want to believe in other beings, some humans cried out for something to worship, it was their nature. Could this woman's daughter be with their prey?

"Okay, just tell us what you know"

"I seen it all, well I thought I had, been around you

know, bikers, punks, god lovers and god haters, Amen to that. She met this man at a bar, smooth talking creep he was, all flash, nice suit with these bright blue come to bed eyes, hell, I would have myself, given the chance, maybe if I were younger. They were sat in this room, thought I was out for the count, but I saw, I saw him drink her blood. You know what, that wasn't the bit that freaked me out, shit her own father was into some real strange shit, no what got me was the look on her face, she was zoned out man, not like I ever saw, even with the H. He was doing something to my girl, I was so scared, even cranked up, I was so freaking scared." Tears were forming in her eyes, her arms and shoulders shaking as she recalled that night.

Richard changed his tune, they might be onto something here, "It's okay, we're here to help, when was this and when was the last time you saw your daughter?" he pulled out a note pad.

"As I said, I been clean nine months now, that night, praise the lord, changed me"

Damn thought Richard, nine months was no good, he should have put two and two together as she told the story, he was about to give up, when she started talking again.

"But I know where she is, some place in the Badlands, over the interstate, North Dakota. I tracked her down last month, someone I know; a drug dealer looking for a back route to Canada, well anyway that's another story, well he saw her. She was shopping for goods, water, toilet rolls, that kind of thing, so I did a little digging. Here." She pulled out a map and promptly pointed to a small town.

For once Bina just sat opened mouth; this was amazing, could this be true, could this be the end of their quest? She felt a tad silly, all their time, efforts and resources only for this junkie to find a hive of them. Richard couldn't contain his smile either, wow, all these years, all this tech and it now looked like an old hippy had blown the whole thing open.

"She up on a compound, in these trees, over this way I think, I know it ain't much but, I just want my baby girl back, she all I got," she added as she blew her nose and sniffed.

"Thank you, this had been very useful, and don't worry we will get your daughter back for you," Richard lied.

As they returned to the car Richard thought of an old story his father had once told him, one about his ancestors tracking down and taking out six of the Sages in one go, he thought about how proud his family would be if he could better that, though he was now feeling more than a little scared as the reality was dawning on him.

Chapter Thirty-Two

1888 AD England

Eric sat in the bar watching from the shadows, hidden from the crowd, waiting, playing with the same drink he had been nursing for over two hours now. This east end public house was quite raucous, filled with sailors, market dealers and whores, the night was getting near the end as was the drinking for most of the people packed inside on this horrible grim foggy night.

Five months ago, he and his team had finally raided Kings college, their mission was to take out the unearthly inhabitants that had lived there for so many years. The information was from the top, as was usual now, and was very detailed and spot on; how many guards, how many doors, who would let them in the gate, which building they had to go to, what they would need and how they would escape. His men were well drilled, and each man knew what they were up against and how important their own part was no matter how small as they assassinated their targets.

These targets were no easy pickings, six in one room could play all sorts of tricks on you, mess with your mind, make the room wobble or collapse, throw tables at you. The good news was they thought they were safe, they were protected, relaxed in their day to day life as they lived on the campus not wanting for anything. The groups had been kept apart from each other for years now and he thought they might not even know they were slowly being wiped out. He doubted the captors would be stupid enough to let them know they were under attack, keep them updated that Edinburgh, Oxford as well as Warminster were no longer, this would freak them out, make them plot to escape; no the creatures might not expect anything but the guards most likely did, if they put up a fight then they would go the same way, it was up to them.

Under the blanket of darkness Eric and eight of his men entered the grounds, three had stayed back covering the exit points. To avoid any unwanted attention the apartment the Sages were kept in was made to look as normal as it could to blend in with the rest of the campus. If you didn't know where to look you could easily pass it by, however, to the trained eye the overly heavy door, barred blacked out windows, and the disguised sentry box for the guards made to look like a store room was a give-away, plus they had inside information, this was where they were hiding, almost in plain sight.

The two guards were taken by surprise and were knocked out cold before they knew what was happening. Eric could tell just by looking at one of them that he wouldn't recover from the bleeding on his head where he had been hit too hard, no time to worry about collateral damage now though.

One man stayed with the now bound, unconscious men to make sure they didn't wake up and sound the alarm, leaving Eric and three more to tackle the Sages. The information had said it was feeding night; these beings only had to eat once week, it was wise to keep them hungry and less powerful from everyone's point of view. That suited tonight's task on two fronts, firstly as an excuse to go into the apartment, secondly their powers would be weakened. Even with the element of surprise, weapons and no escape route it would be dangerous work.

Eric's men grabbed the containers of blood from the sentry box, concealed their guns and found the keys to the apartment. They looked to see if they could disguise themselves in the uniform of the guards but there was no way their clothes would fit any of them; one was a huge man, hands like shovels, his legs must have been twice the size of any of Eric's men's legs - he was the one with the nasty head wound, it needed to have been done like that - the other a string bean overly tall fellow. They would have to hope that it wasn't noticed, they would act quickly as soon as the chance arrived, one thing he knew was the Sages didn't like surprises, they liked to hang back and focus to use the true extent of their power, face to face under pressure, man had the advantage over most of them. He had heard stories of some that were way tougher targets, he hoped for the best this time.

Eric and Jon unlocked the door and entered the apartment whilst the other two stood outside, bayonets attached to their guns. It was a short corridor with doors on either side, they could hear a piano being played in the room on the left, he hoped all six were in there waiting to be fed as he reassuringly felt the revolver in his pocket.

He entered the room, counting four people, one playing the other three standing watching him, backs turned away from the visitors, this was good news, but where were the other two?.

"Ah, dinner time" one said as they turned to acknowledge the two men. Jon, one of Eric's newer men panicked, he dropped the container of blood and immediately started shooting. Having no other choice Eric joined in the volley as they mowed down the four people, their bodies erupting in blood, a chair was transported across the room in a last-ditch attempt of defence to no avail. As the four succumbed to the gun fire the door slammed shut with force, trapping them in the room, Eric instructed Jon to coup-de-grace the Sages as he tried to open the door with no luck. He correctly guessed that the other two, wherever they had been, had sprung into action.

Mary and Emily had been knitting in the room on the right. Hearing the main door open they knew it must be dinner time, by the time they had put down their needles the gun fire had started. They ran for the only exit, but not before blocking the door opposite, slamming it shut and pulling the floorboards up to stop it from being opened. Both in need of blood the activity took its toll on them as they used their powers to force the wooden floor to buckle, to change shape. They turned and ran, they then encountered the other two men outside the entrance, complete with rifles. Emily caused an illusion making the men to start stabbing at imaginary figures as they dodged and slipped by. When they got outside into the fresh air Emily collapsed from the exertion, Mary pulled her friend up and they continued to run.

The three men stationed by the exits saw the two women move past their colleagues and knew by some trickery they had fooled their comrades into fighting an invisible enemy, one man steadied his aim and shot as the other two gave chase.

Mary heard the shot and felt Emily go heavy, she looked at her as she dropped her to the floor, a huge hole in her chest, her dress scarlet red, Mary knew she was done for. She changed direction and went for the wall; she could hear the sound of men running and shouting behind her as a shot pinged past her ears.

Mary was struggling to run in her dress, the men chasing her were making good progress catching up with her. The wall was too high, no way she was getting over, desperate for ideas Mary ran like she had never run before, scanning the view in front for any inspiration, she needed something, anything or she was dead like the others. She had always been quite powerful, more than the others she shared her life with, but she was feeling the drain now as she fought for her very life. She spotted a tree to the far side of the wall and changed course towards it as another shot was fired. Using all the energy she could summon she bent a large bow of the tree, as she got close she jumped on it, stopped using her power and the branch sprang back to its preferred shape taking Mary up with it. She hung on as best she could. That extra ten feet was enough for her to tackle the wall and disappear into the dark London night, she would feed as soon as she could, refill her power, otherwise she knew she would just collapse where she stood.

It had taken Eric and his team five months to finally track her down after her escape. A tale of a blood hungry prostitute had alerted him to this east end public house. Just a story to some, but he knew better than rumours; he was now waiting for her to find a punter and take him somewhere nice, dark and secluded; it would suit her as much as it would suit Eric and his men.

After her escape Mary found herself all alone for the first time in her life, she wasn't old by her own people's standards, but she had always lived under their protection. She was scared, she knew she needed to feed to keep her powers up, it was her only chance of surviving. She walked the streets until she came across The Talbot Arms and witnessed some of the women in there who seem to pick up random men, leave with them and then return a short time later alone. She had heard about these women, they were called ladies of the night, prostitutes who sold their bodies for money. Mary decided that she would become one of these ladies, easy pickings. Tonight, she had picked her latest conquest or meal as he would become, they left the public house and headed for the safe spot she knew.

Eric followed from a safe distance, biding his time. This time she would not be escaping, all exits were covered, by even more men so she couldn't play her tricks.

Mary left the man slumped in the corner, he wouldn't remember a thing when he woke up, most likely blame in on the booze, hopefully, he would think he had hurt his wrist falling over. She felt satisfied and energised; she always did after a feed; then the reality of her situation would creep back into her mind. What was she to do, she couldn't do this forever? She suddenly became aware of the men in the shadows, she knew this wasn't good, she quickly scanned the area for an escape route as she prepared to fight with everything she had.

The fight was vicious, she had kicked like a mule, howled like a banshee, had thrown everything she had at them, controlled two of the men to fight with her for way too short a time, she eventually gave in to the stabbings that were reigning down on her. Eric was in a frenzy as he cut and sliced her apart, even taking out her internal organs. He wasn't going to take any chances on her regenerating. With no saltwater nearby, he wanted to make sure she wasn't coming back from this.

It was total carnage, the noise had attracted too much

attention from passers-by, three of his own men were seriously injured and would need to be taken to hospital for treatment. They had to leave the scene quickly without anyone seeing their faces and being able to identify them, they left the mangled body behind for their own safety, no dissolving this one in the docks.

The papers were all over the murder the next day. It reported that Mary Ann Nichols - it wasn't her real name or the one she had been given at birth all those years ago - a local prostitute had been brutally murdered and butchered. Eric sat in the park next to the man that worked on the inside, the same man who had given them the information all those months ago. "This isn't good, we don't need this heat" he said.

"What do you suggest we do then?" Eric asked. He had completed the mission, all six of the Sages were no more.

After a short pause the man said, "Kill another four or five girls the same way, then stop. We will work with the papers, make out we have a killer on the streets of London, glam it up a bit, the Whitehouse murders or something of that ilk." With that he got up and left, leaving the gruesome task of butchering some more poor sex workers in the same manner with Eric.

There were still people in power who wanted to protect the Sages, thought they were still of some use. Diversion tactics needed to be employed to cover Eric's messy tracks.

Chapter Thirty-Three

2019 AD North Dakota

Marcus finally went to bed. He had taken a young human female with him to his huge luxurious room, this place really was special, but he had fed enough. It had taken nearly all day to drive from Vegas to the compound, but he only really needed to feed properly once a month. Liam, the rent boy, seemed a distant memory, so much had happened so quickly, but his veins were still full.

The girl beside him appeared to be about thirty, perhaps slightly younger. Her arms were scarred from the amount of times she had given her blood, and her eyes seemed distant, almost as if she was brainwashed. She looked at Marcus awestruck, perhaps not believing she was in bed with one of them. Mia had explained the cult-like life these humans lived. They gave themselves freely, or so they thought – he was sure that a little mind control was also in play as he studied them working around the place, doing the various boring tasks.

This made him think, why couldn't they share this planet, alright it wasn't quite the same as drinking cow's milk like the humans did, but there were blood banks, no one needed to be drank from the vein, it could all be done behind closed doors. He knew it couldn't happen though, the humans hated each other, always fighting for control, throw Charles and this lot into the mix as well, he was just as bad as them it seemed, hell bent on winning something unwinnable.

They had brought some Africans over with them, ensuring they brought both male and female, for replenishment purposes, but, over time, most had died. The deaths overtook the birth rate, only a handful of the originals remained. They replaced them with local Americans, nearly exclusively female and all white. Maybe it was the lack of a religious teaching, or maybe it was an upbringing that told them they could be whoever they wanted to be, but it seemed that neither Mexicans nor black people were for this lifestyle.

The tasks the humans were doing couldn't be further from the work his own people were completing. Charles wasn't lying about the tunnels. Underneath the settlement was a huge modern network of tunnels on two levels, leading to bedrooms, cells, bathrooms, lounges and, lastly, the main room on level one, known as the Control Room. This was where they found the others.

There was what seemed an endless array of computers and screens, TVs and monitors, each watched dutifully by one of the team. They all looked so young, Marcus observed – young but devoted – as they watched the channel or website they were assigned to. He was impressed how focused Charles had got them all even if he didn't buy into the overall plan himself. He remembered back to the days in England. Yes, they would do the tasks given, but when left on their own they were, well, just plain lazy. A bit like lions after a kill. Perhaps this purpose and drive that the new, younger leaders had instilled upon them was the reason they were now so successful, why the birth rate had been so fruitful, that in itself wasn't a bad thing.

This was where Marcus had been told he would come into Charles' master plan. He was impressed that Marcus had survived on his own for over a hundred and fifty years. No one else had ever been able to manage that. There had always been at least two of them. Marcus had not only evaded capture, but he had blended in almost completely, using his skills, wit and powers, living in plain sight – no news stories about people going missing, or strange happenings. Charles was in awe and his role for Marcus was to teach these skills to the next generation, as they may have to leave the compound and join the battlefield at some point. Marcus kept his opinion to himself; he didn't mention that he had decided not to kill anyone, just get what he needed, then set them free after wiping their minds.

Marcus had watched them today in their daily tasks, monitoring those screens. He had only been there half an hour, but the news channels showed an ugly picture: a Mosque blown up in Afghanistan, sixty dead; protests in Hong Kong, Barcelona, Venezuela; schoolgirls kidnapped in Africa; a Russian soldier who shot eight of his fellow countrymen; a church on fire in Paris; the Mekong, days away from drought; the rainforest on fire in Brazil; Britain gridlocked by climate protesters, as well as its parliament still frozen over Brexit; a mass shooting, here in America. It was endless, the same every day. Every continent had something bad going on.

Deep in thought, he dismissed the young girl and fell into a much-needed sleep. Tomorrow, Charles had promised to tell him all the details, the grand plan, he would see where he sat on that once told in full. There was something about the glorious leader he wasn't warming to, he would keep his cards close to his chest for the time being, relax for once and take the offerings with pleasure.

Chapter Thirty-Four

1941 AD – Germany

Following orders, Matthew had continued working with the Germans. For the past five years, he and his team had been inspiring the party with battle tactics and inventions, war inventions. His own personal project was the Uranprojekt, also known as Germany's nuclear programme. He had helped a couple of years earlier with the fission element, but things had slowed down when half the team, mostly physicists, were taken away to help with the war effort after invading Poland.

The leaders in the party were idiots. If they had left the team with him, they would now have the bomb which Babock had seen in the vision. Matthew was now working with just a handful of men. He knew nothing himself, but his task was to stay well fed and focus the scientists' minds.

Today seemed a bit odd, though, he thought. There seemed to be a larger military personnel presence than usual. Perhaps a visit on their progress was scheduled by some top brass. The scientists appeared to be on edge and kept looking at Matthew and his two comrades, Erica and Phillip.

Matthew had left Babock as they went their separate ways forty years ago. They had predicted the war, but it didn't play out as they saw. A confused Matthew set to his task and wasn't really surprised when battle commenced once again. This wouldn't have seemed a long gap between the wars, even by human standards, never mind his own.

They may have got the first result wrong, but their plans and meddling ensured it wasn't too long before fighting started again. Babock had told them that all-out war and annihilation of most of the humans was the only way forward for his people. They had to take humans back to a few wandering tribes around the world.

Anyway, back to work, he thought. Must be feeding time soon, he hoped.

Group Commander Alfred Benz of the SS studied the room. So, these three beings were the special ones, the ones from Persia. They don't look that special, he thought, noticing their dirty tanned skin. He hadn't seen one before, unlike his comrades in the mountains who had found that weird small enclave. Apparently the stupid French had hidden them there when things had turned against them in the constant wars with the English, many, many years ago. Fools, he uttered under his breath. It turned out they were happy to be found and wanted to get involved again. Boredom gets to everyone, in the end.

It was quite by chance that the team that found them realised who was helping the party in Berlin. If that one man hadn't been on that expedition, then Alfred would not be here today, about to execute his orders.

A Jewish rabbi, of all the people had been caught in the pass trying to escape, he had been there when they had stumbled upon the lost French tribe, he had told the story of these people, these blood drinkers who had shaped mankind. He told everything he had learnt and read about these ancient beings from the oldest of manuscripts found in Jerusalem. The Jews had kept this knowledge to themselves over the years, much to the annoyance of everyone else. However, things change when facing a firing squad. In a desperate attempt to save himself and the lives of his family, the rabbi thought it best to tell the Nazis everything he knew, become useful to them. It didn't work, as they put a bullet in his head, along with his entire family that was with him at the time, as soon as they understood his tale. Couldn't have him telling of the Nazis' find, could we?

So, it had been decided: the command had total faith in the project, with or without these "helpers." There were too few of them to make a real difference in the war effort and everything was going well, anyway. The eleven found in the mountains would be put with these five, here in Berlin, and they would be shipped to the Ukraine, where Dr Mengle could do some experiments on them. Hitler wanted to see what made them tick, along with some other occult initiative they were looking into, they wanted to see how or if the master race could breed with them and create an unstoppable soldier. With the Aryans' true blood and the powers of these beings combined, the war would be won and then the world would be theirs.

Matthew saw the men come in and at first assumed that they were bringing in blood that he was now craving. It had been over two weeks since his last feed and he was feeling in need of sustenance. Perhaps that was why the project was stalling. As he pondered this, the explosion of gunfire brought him to his senses. He saw Erica and Phillip collapse as their kneecaps were shot through. He didn't have time to think as the bullets reached him, inflicting the same pain and injury as the bullets ripped through his soft flesh and muscle until they shattered the bone that lay inside.

Alfred ordered his men to handcuff, bind and blindfold their new captives, shouting, "What are you looking at? Get on with your work!" to the astonished physicists as he and his men promptly left the lab with Matthew, Erica and Phillip.

Matthew and his comrades were never seen again.

Chapter Thirty-Five

1945 AD – North Dakota

Charles was fuming as he sat alone in his room. How could he have got it so wrong – so wrong he had lost the lives of some of his best people, ones he trusted to do his bidding away from the safety of the tribe, as well as wasting precious time? He thought back to that night in Africa, that night when they all foresaw the events of the future, the atomic bomb.

It was his own overconfidence that set their plan in motion. Success after success had made him arrogant. He was so sure that Germany would prevail and finish what they had started those twenty-two years earlier. They had all seen the vision, but he alone chose the plan. He felt like he had played his cards too soon.

He now knew what they had seen was the Americans testing the bomb on their own land – Arizona, of all places. This had confused Charles into backing the wrong side.

Perhaps if Matthew's team had been successful with

their project in Germany, it would have been different. The powers they had used to foresee the future did show a vision from the future; however, he had read it wrong. It showed that this magic was both unpredictable and dangerous. He now made the decision to never invest so much energy and planning in that power again. It had cost them dearly.

His spies had informed him of Matthew's plight. How, like the Jews, they were rounded up and sent away, never to come back. The Nazis had gone mad. Instead of using the talents of his men, they sought to recreate them, mix the races and create a new super species. He shuddered when he thought of the torture and pain they must have all suffered as that madman had experimented on them.

Germany and its allies were all but defeated and he knew that Japan would soon follow. If America had made a weapon like he had seen in the vision, he was damn sure they were going to use it.

This war had cost millions of lives, but not enough. The annihilation was nowhere near the amount needed for his kind, his plan. After two world wars, the humans had failed to bomb themselves back to the Stone Age as he had hoped they would, even with these new super weapons. He needed the humans to be back to wandering tribes, so he could rise up and rule them like he had back in Africa, but it wasn't going to happen anytime soon.

He felt defeated. Even after the war, the population

would be over two billion, and he knew after such devastation there would be a baby boom. It always happened; it was like they knew they had to replenish, breed more babies to go off and die in another man's land.

He was the leader, the group all looked up to him. At least he still had that on his side, there was no one questioning his authority. They had followed him against the elders all those decades ago and he hadn't let them down. He was now unsure where they were headed, there was no escape left in the entire world where they would be safe – well, safe and where they would have enough food to keep them going.

They needed humans to feed off, yet he sensed that these humans were there to wipe his people out. Mass death just wasn't going to work, so now he needed a new plan. He thought back to the older empires – what would be seen by man now as ancient. What was it the Romans said? 'Divide and Conquer.' Perhaps that was the way, his people's only chance.

Chapter Thirty-Six

2019-AD Washington

The meeting had been going on for hours. A trusted representative from each US agency was in the room along with people from the UK, France and Italy. They may all have worked for the various law enforcement departments, but their true loyalties were to the cause, all members here worked for Raven. This was the underground organisation's name that had infiltrated most if not all the power bases in the western world. The name being taken from Arthur Raven, a man who had worked tirelessly and behind the backs of his own government hundreds of years ago to try and wipe out the Sages. Only a few people worked directly for Raven, the others took their pay cheque from the tax man.

The old foes China and Russia had been discussed at length - Russia's alleged meddling in western affairs from vote rigging to assassinations on foreign soil, mixed in with China's south sea expansion, tension with its neighbours, aggressive land grabbing in Australia and Africa, the treatment of minorities and the wests increasing reliance on cheap imported goods - it didn't paint a pretty picture and the old western powers were worried, not the easy come easy go presidents and prime ministers, the real people who ran the world.

The men and women who were gathered here mainly wanted to return to being the world players, some in truth wanted revenge for past deeds against their families, but most, wanted to be in charge, pulling the strings, like it used to be. Things had slipped over the past decades, too much power had swapped hands and they knew they were being played by a force based in their own lands that wanted to not only cripple them but destroy their way of life. The enemy wanted to dismantle western civilisation, erase the history and start again in the chaos, once this was done they would move onto the rest of the world.

There had been a backlash after the world wars, some in England thought that things would have gone better if they still had the power of the Sages to harness and swing the tide their way. They craved for the glory days of their forefathers, after all, the vote had gone that way, but they had been betrayed and over the years these hit squads aided and abetted by inside men had killed off any Sages in the empire. The Raven group had been lucky not to have been wiped out themselves, but as the cold war became the main focus they were forgotten about as much as the Sages themselves.

That brought them to today's main topic which wasn't

totally unrelated to the mornings review of China.

"Look, we all know these things have been eating away, plotting against us for the entire last century. We know that a large unknown group was based in Africa, ones that had missed the clearance in the UK then Europe, we know they are rich, ruthless, resourceful and committed. What we don't know is how many of our leaders are in bed with them, or what their end game is."

"I disagree, we know exactly what their end game, as you put it, is. They want to eliminate us, our achievements, our cities, our way of life, once they have made us all weak they will endorse a war with Russia, China or both. Our leaders will not give up even knowing we couldn't win in a straight shoot out, full scale nuclear war will happen, leaving them to crawl out from the stone they are hiding under and take control," the old Englishman stated in a huffy tone, acting as if he had heard it all before.

"We have tried shutting down the payments, limit their influence but it's like pushing water uphill. Every site we shut down ten more pop up almost overnight, they have spread confusion and discontent all over the west and we are still no closer to locating their base of operations, these are not lone wolf cell tactics," an FBI man responded.

"Ah, but we are closer than you think. I have news we have narrowed them down, not quite the exact location, but my field agents will know in the next week, maybe less. We think this is a total hive, sixty to seventy in the one place, running everything from there."

The room was stunned, everyone had their own theory of how or where the Sages were set up, but no one thought it would be that many, perhaps a cell of six to ten scattered around; this news was massive. If anyone else had said it they wouldn't have believed it, but Harold Marksman was the expert, his family alone had ridded England of the pests without anyone finding out and also without damaging British interests at the time.

"What do you know?" asked Diana Reagan, a top CIA commander.

Diana had found herself involved with Raven after the Vietnam War, not that she knew anything about these people before, but her boyfriend at the time had changed so much; one moment he was a good, clean-living American boy, patriotic, then overnight, becoming a leading activist on campus. He started just by saying and stating things he had never showed any interest in before. Changing from wanting to be a law enforcement officer, like all his family before him, to this radical revolutionist that hated the country of his birth. He wasn't the only one, the American youth were changing in lots of ways at that time. They had met through their mutual interest in law enforcement and both wanting to pursue that career; she was now confused and even scared by this change in him. Concerned at his complete U turn, fearing the worst, she had followed him one night to one of his meetings. Afterwards he had met this mysterious woman, at first she suspected he was having an affair, some beautiful like-minded student poisoning his thoughts, however, when she saw this woman, she noticed that she was so much older, she looked like she could have been his grandma. Diana kept her distance and watched; she could tell by his body language he was besotted with this older woman. Was she a Russian spy? This sort of thing was all over the papers at the time, she decided to investigate some more.

She would listen intently as he spoke, letting him think she was on his side, pretending to be intrigued, she told him she wanted to follow this path he was now on. She felt no remorse lying to him, feeding his obsession, he had betrayed her and their country. She watched him become a puppet for that woman. He was at the forefront of a demonstration outside the Pentagon, where he was beaten so badly by US Marshalls and soldiers that had had enough of all the protests that he ended up in hospital. Diana visited him in the hospital and after seeing his broken body, decided she had seen enough, she was going to take matters into her own hands.

She knew where this woman lived with her husband; that was odd Diana thought, husband and boyfriend? It confirmed she was a foreign agent in her mind, either that or these new hippy types didn't live the American way. Diana took her dad's hunting rifle and waited outside this woman's house.

After a short while she saw the woman leaving the house, Diana shouted to grab her attention, the woman turned and starred. Diana was suddenly overcome by a strange sensation, those eyes transfixed on her, she was frozen to the spot, her head was telling her to shoot this traitor, but she found herself unable to do a damn thing. The woman slowly walked towards her smiling, her beautiful blue eyes staring into the depths of her very soul, she suddenly knew what Dwight had seen in her. Instead of shooting her like she had planned she started to feel emotionally connected to her, she couldn't help herself, she wasn't that kind of girl, she had never had feelings for another woman. She felt herself surrendering to this woman and began to drop the gun just as a shot fired out from the darkness.

The woman dropped to her knees, injured but still alive. Diana snapped back to her senses. She saw a man come out of the shadows brandishing a sword of all things; the shooter was still on the other side of the road. He took a swing of the sword and tried to decapitate the downed women, he missed and shouted "Bollocks" in an accent that told Diana he wasn't from around here. The woman, one hand holding her side, held her free hand up, screamed something and a drain cover flew up from the street and hit the attacker square on his head, knocking him down.

Another shot from across the road hit its target again, but this didn't stop her from regaining her composure, she managed to get up and limped across the road towards him. Diana couldn't believe what she was seeing, but she knew she needed to act, to do something. What she did know was that this woman had some sort of powers and was dangerous, much more so than she could have imagined.

She picked up the dropped sword and charged full pelt towards the woman, running it straight through her, who once again screamed, this time falling into a crumpled heap onto the ground. The rifle man came running across the road and smashed the butt of his rifle into her head, caving it in, Diana, dropped the bloodied weapon, threw up and then promptly passed out.

That was the start of her involvement with Raven. She woke up in the back of the car of the two men that had saved her, she shuddered to think what would have happened if they hadn't been so close by, tracking this woman. Questions had been asked by both sides, that night. The two Englishmen that had rescued her from gods knows what had made sure she was okay before letting her go, but she was on a mission now, more determined than ever to find the truth.

As the years past and her career in the force took off, she carried on her mission to find out what was going on in the world, she soon found she was not the only one pissed off at the interference in the war, her eyes had been opened to a whole new world. The agency that the two Englishmen were from kept tabs on her and followed her career, she was eventually contacted some 15 years later and recruited to Raven.

Back in the room she waited for the English guy to answer her question, his accent reminding her of the very first time she had heard one.

"The Vegas thing, well it may be closer to home than we thought, got my nephew and his Mossad agent friend on it. I have good intel we may be finally onto them; we need to review our resources and think this through properly; a - we don't want another Waco, b - they cannot escape. If we don't stop their meddling, this country is doomed, Europe will follow and then let there be no doubt China will attack. Without using our bombs our armies will be too weak, either by foolish politicians unable to act or divided cities and chaos."

Each person left knowing their role, they had to mobilise the troops, the news channels, the politics, the plan, all had to be completed in secret. Red herrings, fake accounts, mislaid orders, scams, ruses and lies all had to be in place if they were to take this to the enemy. If it got out what they were planning then the chance would be lost, they all knew their very future depended on finding this rot, this cancer that was messing everything up and finally make these age-old beasts vanish once and for all.

David Geller walked with purpose to his car, nervously checking over his shoulder to ensure no one was following him or in hearing distance, he got in and started the engine, pulled out his phone, well, his second phone, and dialled a number, it rang a few times before a soft voice answered.

Diana watched the tall awkward man cross the car park from where she stood on top of the office block, she could tell by his movement he was not at ease, the tip off from one of her friends over in DEA that he couldn't be trusted might be paying dividends, she may do worse than get some of her resources to keep a close eye on this man.

"It's me," he said, "listen, I just finished a meeting, you might want to warn your friends over in the Badlands, we are onto them," he hung up, checked again to make sure no one was around, had he done the right thing? Would she even act on the information he had given her? Would he be found out? He put the car in gear and headed off to the hospital, hoping for the breakthrough that had been promised in his daughter's illness.

Senator Illihad put the phone down, this wasn't good news, the people he spoke off had been very helpful in her campaign, not only with funds but quite resourceful in keeping her enemies at bay. She knew one day she would have to return a favour, not that they had asked her to, but she knew it was just how these things worked, you scratch my back, I scratch yours. All politics was like that, it was why nothing ever really changed, by the time you got into power you had called in so many favours your hands were tied. If you wanted to stay where you were you had to look after your friends, she had hoped this group was different, perhaps they were, that was why they hadn't requested anything of her, but she felt the right thing was to warn them.

She decided she wouldn't tip them off just yet, the information may be flawed, it was always better to have two sources, she would do some more digging, a one-off comment from a bent DEA agent wasn't enough to panic yet, no matter how he bragged about his connections. She sat there and thought of her options. Who else would be in the know? That CIA woman owed her a favour after she had given them information on Yemen, her country of birth, for the Saudis. Now what was she called, she flicked through her files until she found Diana Reagan details, yes that was her, she wondered if she would be able to fill in any gaps, re-affirm the tip.

Chapter Thirty-Seven

2019 AD – North Dakota

Marcus had slept well for once, maybe due to the size of the bed in this luscious room, or simply that he was tired from the previous day's events he guessed as he yawned and stretched out his aching limbs. After showering, again impressed at the equally grand modern design, he joined Charles, Mia and three others of his kind, that he hadn't met before, on the decking area of the complex. It was a beautiful day – a cold breeze, but not a cloud in the sky, he hoped he could keep up with all the name changes, he didn't want to look foolish, he was glad he hadn't had to change his, not ever.

"How are you, Marcus? I know old people don't sleep too well," Charles teased.

Marcus noted that he always seemed to be in a good mood, always joking, why not he thought, this place, the set up was amazing, life looked good, maybe too good!

"Now you are fully rested and safely away from that

sinful city of Vegas, let me bring you up to date," he continued. "As you can see, we have it pretty good here, tucked away out of sight of the rest of the world, but we keep our eyes on them, don't we?" He addressed the others who all nodded knowingly.

Marcus didn't know if he was supposed to say anything or ask any questions at this point. Charles was a little too smug, he thought, over-confident, Marcus was too long in the tooth to under -estimate the humans, time and time again they had bettered him and his kind. Let's hear the messiah out, though, Mia has faith in him, and he did reunite us, after all.

"So, you went AWOL in what, the late 1800s? Mia has already told you about Africa, so, let's see – right, where is a good place to start. Let's begin with the error: we used the dreaded foresight as the colonial powers descended upon us in Africa, and a great war was seen, ending in America, with them losing after atomic bombs were launched."

Charles paused for a moment; his cheeriness vanished as he recalled his error that led to the deaths of many of his kind, including his close confident and friend, Matthew. He felt incredible sorrow knowing his plans had sent his trusted friend to a horrible death at the hands of the Nazis. He was glad they lost in the end, after that, even if it didn't fit on with his plans.

"What I had seen, what I had wrongly seen, was the damn stupid Americans testing their bombs in their own country, bloody Arizona, not those worthless Nazis winning the war." His anger showed as he spat out the sentence. He looked upwards, focusing on something the others could not see.

For the first time since they had arrived, everyone was deadly serious. They had all been jovial up until now.

Charles continued: "So the war wiped out millions. With both wars combined, it was about a hundred and twenty million I think, but they just kept going. Even after the wars, they were up to over two billion people. We had to change our tactic; all-out war just wasn't working. Coupled with how they could now create new inventions on their own, if we were to survive – and by that I mean live properly, not just feed on scraps, having to hide – no, to thrive, we needed to break them.

"America was the new superpower. The old ones were done for, their empires slowly but surely breaking up. We needed to hurt America.

"It didn't take long for these paranoid bloodthirsty fools to carry on the slaughter, although now, with these bombs, it changed the game again. Instead of invading and fighting the locals, the superpowers played out wars by proxy, playing their games safely, miles away, sticking their noses in. Well, that gave us an idea: if they could do that, so could we. We had plenty of wealth from our mining days, plus we didn't need any of it to live. We also had our spells and tricks, so, no matter what they could do, we could do better.

"It wasn't long before we had a chance to try out our new tactics. Vietnam was a powder keg, just waiting to explode on the world. I bet most people in the west couldn't point it out on a map, but they soon would.

"Vietnam wasn't lost on the battlefields of South East Asia, it was lost in the lounges of America, or something like that. 'Television!' We worked twofold: half of us worked on the media, questioning the politicians, and stirring up trouble on campuses all over the country, whilst the other half worked on weapons and the Senate passing laws, sending troop after troop into a hopeless war they knew from the start they couldn't win. 'Television!' I would like to claim that invention on behalf of our people, but I think they came up with that on their own," he paused, just for a moment as he thought about if they had over played their hand, exposed themselves when they really didn't need to, would their lives be different now if they hadn't become so involved? Things had changed after that war not only for the humans but his kind, still it needed to be done if they were to ever rule again, he quickly gathered his train of thought, a faint heart never fucked a fair maiden.

"That war hurt America and still does – its ghost plays a part in every conflict they have been involved in since. Seeing how we managed to successfully divide the country with propaganda, anti-propaganda, lies, truths, highlighting things, hiding other things, we knew this was the way forward. Starting with America, we placed ideas all over the world, conflicting ideas: Marxist theory, rebels, freedom fighters, terrorists. Depending whose side you were on, civil unrest multiplied."

"As the eighties came, we worked on changing laws.

We made gambling accessible, we looked to change the law on gay marriages, access to porn, abortion, civil rights, all things that made man's world work. Things that enabled them to live the life they wanted in their nice cities far from war and then ….?" His smile was now broadly returning.

"And?" Marcus asked, as if on cue.

"They went and invented the internet!" he replied excitingly.

The others, including Mia, all laughed, Marcus didn't, to him this proved that mankind didn't need them anymore, they had evolved, taken the lead. Was this a sign that their time was over? No one noticed he didn't join in.

"What a godsend that was. Now, as you have seen, we can influence, cajole, train them. We were quite apt at it by now, but even we weren't prepared for this. I mean, Niles even set up suicide sites – sites that talk people into taking their own lives. You couldn't make it up. Well, you could – we did! Those fools. What a move," he was laughing now, on a well-practised roll, and the others were loving it.

"We fed their obsession – yes, the destruction of the family unit. You see them on their phones all the time – at meals, concerts, even when they are in the gym. In the past, fads were for teenagers – new fashion, new inventions – they were for the young, but this thing, this was for everyone, every age. It was endless, even better than television, which still has an important part to play.

"Yes, it was genius. We just sat back and watched as they stared at those screens. When they invented the telegraph or even the television, it was to communicate, educate and inform, keep them up to speed. Now, if you don't watch the news, you are uninformed; if you do, you are misinformed," Charles said in a self-congratulatory way, as he looked around the room, the mood somewhat lightened again.

"Fake news! Fake news!" Niles shouted, as he rolled around laughing.

"We tried annihilation, but it didn't quite work out, so we moved onto civil war, although there was nothing civil about it. Not north against south, like Vietnam, Korea, America. Nations used to fight nations, the whole country united by a common cause – a race, a religion, independence, morals, whatever. Now, well, we are well on the way. We think, by 2050, or even sooner for some, each country will be just that: a meaningless borderline on the globe."

"No more a country united; rich vs. poor, white vs. black, religion vs. religion – even the same ones fighting the same ones, like the stupid Arabs. It's working already: gay vs. straight, feminist vs. trans, old vs. young, country dwellers vs. city folk, all the gender confusion. I could continue. We just need to keep stoking the fires sit back and watch them all burn as they eat each other up."

"What then?" Marcus asked. He could see the world around him had changed over the years – strip clubs, gambling dens, swingers' parties, drug wars, rapes, paedophile grooming gangs, this movement, that movement, every bloody movement, protests every week about something, mass migration.

"You look like you can't see it? Europe is a mess. The steady influx of Africans will do them; they can't cope, we have been spending some money in the right areas, helping out. We have them thinking it's all good; we have taught the younger generation they can be anything they want to be – music, dancing, stunts – no real talent, just watch and consume.

"We have taught them to worship totally irrelevant talentless fools – not great generals or explorers, scientists who found cures to horrible diseases that plagued them. No, they idolise some idiot that looks good in a dress on a night out or a bikini on a superyacht– and they don't even look that good; it's all filters and fake, anyway.

"The west is being told they need younger foreign people to come in and take care of them, they haven't thought what happens when these imports get old themselves. British people alone have aborted eight million babies since the law changed; kids are growing up brainwashed about climate change, thinking they will not have babies in order to save the planet; we have made men obsessed with porn, no longer happy with their own women. No stigma attached, it is so easy to access anywhere you are, even on your phone! Or worse, they're obsessed with themselves, becoming vegan, more bothered about their hair or beards, becoming weak. They may have abs, but they are no longer warriors.

"The gay community is eating themselves alive and tying themselves up in knots. Every time something happens or changes, we spark them off in another direction until they are totally unsure what they do actually want or even who they actually are. As one law is conceded, we just move them on to the next one, continually outraged, winding up the straight people. No. Europe, America, Canada and Australia – all the Western countries, my friend, are fucked."

"It's not just Europe, though. What about the rest of the world?" Marcus asked, trying to get a word in.

"Look, Europe, America – that was the first target. We finish them off, learn from that. Where America leads, the rest follow. Look at Hong Kong right now; China is pissing off everyone else in the region with its sea expansion, something we have been helping with. I think we may see armed conflict over that way soon, and the west will be so weakened by inner turmoil, they won't play a part, as we have crippled their democracies. Their elected are just weak self-centred fools, more concerned with votes than actually doing any good. They are paralysed, unable to do anything as they all want different things. We just poke our noses in when needed, prompt the debate so much that nothing really gets done.

"If that's not enough, we have droughts, tidal waves, famine, disease – there are so many overpopulated cities in the east, it doesn't take much. A new pandemic, perhaps, things we can help move along. We still have a few tricks up our sleeves – or we can use our wealth to cripple them.

"Social justice, white privilege, white guilt – these are all our little ploys. Remember, we used to befuddle someone with a spell, confuse the hell out of them – no need anymore. For every story online, there are ten opposite ones. Is the world round? Well, of course it is. Hold on, a few taps on a computer and bang, someone here says it's flat. It's madness!

"If you think something and look it up, you will find thousands that are like-minded, making you think you are right no matter how absurd your thinking is! You can live in your own echo chamber whichever side of whatever argument you are on.

"That's what our team are doing right now, downstairs in the control room. We watch, we listen and we stoke. If someone needs a helping hand, then we fund them. It doesn't matter which side, left or right, right or wrong, as long as it's causing conflict then it's job done, that protest the other day, we funded the posters and banners for both sides, came out of the same factory press place" he laughed.

Marcus sat there and took it all in. Charles had a plan and it looked like he had the resources to implement it, but why, was this really needed, he was acting so over the top like a movie villain, a power crazy mad man, it just wasn't needed, they had the power to actually help the world, the whole world, if they did that he was sure a blind eye could be turned by the bloodletting couldn't it, all the fighting, all the time, couldn't it just end?

He digested what had just been said, time was always on his people's side – forty or fifty years was nothing to them – but could this happen? Surely the humans would wake up at some point. The last wars cost so much life and confusion, the world still suffered with it today, as the powers re-grabbed what they could, if only for a short time. Borders were changed to suit, puppets installed to tow the Western agenda, but it didn't last. The world was a mess, but no matter how many died in war, or millions in the aftermath, they kept breeding.

"So, what do you think, old man?" Charles asked. A smile at his own brilliance beaming on his tanned face. "You have been around longer than us, apart from Mia. Will the chimps continue to fall into my trap?"

Marcus thought long and hard, ignored the old man comment, he wasn't sure if he was just saying it because he was older or was trying to make another point, show his dominance in some way, he was silent for a few minutes as they all looked towards him. He had seen so many changes over the years, but one thing he knew was that mankind liked to breed and equally liked to fight. So many changes, so many power bases and empires that had come and gone even just in his time, how many countless ones before he was born, he was still in shock at the events of the last two days, he needed time to think, alone, work it out for himself, he decided to buy some time.

"Their history is a lie, yet I see no reason why their

future should hold any truth either." He said summing up what he thought they wanted to hear, rather than what he was truly thinking.

With that, he raised his glass, the entire room followed suit and raised their glasses too, grinning away, Marcus wasn't so sure though, was Charles' hospitality to him genuine?, or was it that maybe he had lived in the shadows too long, too long on his own, fending for himself, watching the world pass him by and change, the set up here was great, amazing really, but was it wise to try and dominate the world, poke the bear, could a handful really take on literally billions?, or should they, as Marcus thought, be happy with their lot and live out their days in this splendour, truth was he was here now, with his sister, their kin, he only wished he felt safer than he did, like he did in his small simple little house in the Vegas suburbs.

Chapter Thirty-Eight

2019 AD Colorado

Richard and Bina sat in the hotel restaurant awaiting the food they had ordered, apart from a travelling salesman type propping the bar up, they were the only other customers, he was well out of ear shot. Bina faced the front door whilst Richard could view the kitchen, they were seated far enough away from either entrance should anyone else enter, both were carrying concealed side arms.

The precautions were common practice, but tonight they felt even more sensible than usual, they knew they were close, they also knew not to underestimate their enemy, too many agents had been taken out in the past just as they had closed in. This latest murder case and missing person just seemed to fit right into the whole scenario. Were they finally, after hundreds of years so close, they could both feel it? Richard himself had never actually seen one, not that he knew of anyway, but he knew all about them, it was in his blood, his family duty, he had been told this as he grew up. Bina had taken three out in two separate incidents, once she relaxed she liked retelling the stories but only to Richard. Working together they had built up a really close relationship, she loved his Englishness, he, her bravery and commitment, there was nothing sexual in the pairing just mutual respect and determination, neither would have wanted anyone else as a partner. She reminded him of the agent in NCIS, Ziva, slightly older, same build, same commitment and generally in looks as well; the main difference the burn scar on Bina's neck, not from a heroic battle but play time when she was young; it added to her persona of a hard arse. She reminded him of the TV star so much he often called her Zebra as a joke, she didn't get it, much like the character, but he liked it.

"So, we had information about this engineer, a Canadian, in Brussels. He was making a supergun for Iraq, trying to kick off another war in the nineties. He was inspired, we believed, by his lover, this blue-eyed woman that had turned up out of nowhere. Anyway, he was too clever for his own good, we raided the place, shot him and took the woman we found there, she went for a swim that night, her body never washed up to the shore. He was my first kill, it's scary, you know, I was only in my late teens, you never know what to expect, I shot him, he was human, he died there in the apartment. The woman, you see them but even after all the training you never know what they could do, to be honest I'm not sure I truly believed, but when you see them you know.

"She never tried anything, well not that we knew she just pleaded for her life, denied any knowledge, perhaps that was a spell, trying to confuse us, we knew she was real as she melted in the water, like the wicked witch of the north."

"West, Zebra, it was wicked witch of the west," Richard corrected her. Hearing this story put him deep in thought. What if this was a huge nest? What could they conjure up? Did the good guys stand a chance? They had been planning this event for years, always updating their arsenal for such a day, he was sure of one thing though, the element of surprise was crucial, tomorrow him and Bina were on a reconnaissance mission using drones to check out three areas where this compound could be.

Bina, over dessert then told of the other two they had captured then dispatched found living in Lebanon. They didn't seem to be trying to the take over the world, maybe they were a sleeper cell, but rumours of strange goings on and the disappearance of a few children had led her and her team there. A car bomb had blown their legs off as they started the engine before the team swooped in and finished the job by severing their heads to ensure no resurrection, no one took any notice of car bombs in that part of the world, the next day was if it had never happened.

An FBI place in Denver had been put aside for them to use and monitor the drones. They were full Raven members, agents, they didn't have any distractions like so many others in the organisation, they just borrowed what they needed, when they needed it, leaving it to the higher ups to provide the cover story and resource for them.

If it hadn't been for the blatant meddling in Vietnam, the world and more importantly the USA, would have forgotten the Sages and all they had done and could do by now. They would have been seen like the dinosaurs and written off in the history books, although very secret ones. The way they influenced that war woke up a lot of powerful people that they were still out there, this time working for themselves and their own interests, they had made important people aware of their existence, not only important but dangerous people.

Richard had gone from practically a lone investigator to head witch hunter, he had been on the verge of giving up, finally believing that his enemy had gone from this world when he had received the call from his uncle. Some people wanted to speak to them, help them, he had never looked back, and now, tomorrow they were using drones to check out three compounds, one of which may be housing the biggest haul of the enemy since the height of the British empire, he had to admit, he was equally excited as he was petrified.

Chapter Thirty-Nine

2019 AD North Dakota

Marcus was visiting the nursery, he had never seen so much young life of his kind in all his years, Mia was his guide for today. The complex seemed never ending, room after room. Although enough above ground, the tunnels, that was another world all together, two levels of activity. He could tell as she showed off the impressive area she was thinking of her own baby, the joy she was expecting to come.

However, this wasn't a free stay, everyone had to play their part, earn their living. Marcus was expected to give a speech this afternoon, using his experience to teach some "teenagers" how to blend in, not get noticed. This was a real issue as most had never left the compound or interacted with normal people. Marcus had found that most he had spoken to since being here had a strange accent, not recognisable American in anyone's books, more a hybrid of South African - he guessed from the years the adults had lived in that area and coupled in a strange way with the way people spoke on the TV - to Marcus it sounded odd and was a tell-tale sign he thought if anyone was looking out for anything out of the ordinary. In Vegas there were hundreds of accents, most of the workers would just know you were not an American, that's one of the reason he had moved there. He lost count of the number of people he had heard saying any Englishman they met was Australian, but go anywhere else that wasn't a tourist trap, off the well beaten tracks, you would be questioned on your heritage, he thought that would be a lesson he should give.

He also picked up on the language used, one of his strengths had been to move with the times, use modern terms, fit in, you didn't want to stand out talking like a servant from a period drama if you were supposed to be a farmer from Kentucky or an activist from New York.

These were his first thoughts when Charles had first explained how he thought Marcus could add some benefit to the cause. Playing along until he gathered his inner thoughts about the whole project he followed Mia across the courtyard to the room designated for teaching.

He stopped as he thought he saw a glint of light in the sky, way up beyond normal vision.

"What's up?" Mia asked as she noticed he had stopped, her gaze following his upward.

He wasn't sure, was it a plane jetting off somewhere, that didn't seem right, no vapour trail, he squinted, there was definitely something up there, a drone perhaps, this worried him.

"This usual?" he asked his sister pointing to where he saw the light.

"Yeah, perhaps. I know," she replied as she focussed on something for a short while, a breeze quickly brought over a large rain cloud that now ruined the clear blue sky of moments before, "there you go, happy now?" she grinned.

Marcus was concerned, it all was just too easy he thought, it wasn't like Mia to be slack, they continued on to the classroom.

Richard sat looking at the screen, the drone information had already provided a result, one of the areas they were looking at was surrounded by hemp crops, this was great as it had justified the use of the drone that day, the DEA would be informed duly when it suited him.

That left two, each could be the place they were looking for, one registered as a training college, the other a farmstead. He and Bina watched the footage as it was live streamed to them, neither of them sure which was the most favourable target; that was until they saw two people cross the courtyard of the training college. They had been watching the surrounding fields where a handful of workers were farming the land, or maintaining it, they had zoomed in to look to if they could get any facial recognition, as they did this the two new people looked upwards, in seconds a cloud had obscured their view.

They both looked at each other, that was too handy, far too convenient. Even before the computer spat out the information that one of the workers in the field via facial recognition was identified as a missing person named Starlight they knew this was the place they had been looking for, it was showtime.

Chapter Forty

2020 AD North Dakota

"Okay, thanks for the heads up." Charles hung the phone up, that was food for thought, it had confirmed his suspicions, the old enemies were drawing closer, this information re-enforced his stance, he was doing the right thing, the world needed to erupt and soon, traitors would be dealt with.

He sat in his large personal quarters alone, things had panned out well overall, his tribe had done nothing but prosper for the last seventy years after the Nazi error, but his people were still so few, hiding from the outside world. Living here they had no complaints, but Charles wanted more, he wanted it all, it was his destiny. His mission was to reset the balance, his promise to his people to put them back at the top of the food chain, their rightful place.

He was confident that all the work they had been doing over these years was poised ready to be used at short notice, the humans he had in place to protect them wouldn't do anything to upset their bank accounts, their voting blocks and power bases until it was too late. Once again man's rivalry would be their downfall, always fighting each other, always trying to conquer each other.

He needed to take the information he had just received to the table, inform the others, his trusted circle. That was what true leadership was about, making the team think they were involved in the decision making, tell them enough, just enough to agree with you, then they feel infused, committed, not that he had any problems on that front, they were a loyal flock, they loved him, border line worshipped him, in his mind he had earnt their loyalty. He had led them away at the right time, it may have been years in the making but he knew a purge would come, the northern tribes were no more, nothing ever came out of Asia or South America that sounded like his peoples doing, expeditions had found no one, this was it now, the last tribe he feared. He left to gather the others; plans needed to be put into place.

Diana, let her phone ring out, she wanted to be somewhere private for this conversation. She excused herself from the meal she was enjoying with her friends and went outside, the weather was a typical February evening, thankfully dry but bitterly cold as anyone would expect in Denver, she made her way across the road to the park and settled under a streetlight.

"Senator, how can I help you?" she asked as the call was immediately answered.

"Hi, Diana, thanks for getting back to me so quickly," Senator Illihad replied. "I know it's late, so I'll be brief, just need you to confirm something for me, something to do with our friends. I hear they might get a late Christmas present, someone popping in to see them, is that correct?"

"Yes, I can confirm" Diana hung up, it was way too cold out here for any formalities, besides she had another couple of equally important calls to make.

"We have a traitor; Niles please despatch a team to Wyoming. Make it look normal, no scrap that, something special, let's send a message to any other potential turn coat. Have the team get on the way but let me think of what we can actually do, use Lydia, she's good and strong" Charles said.

Marcus was confused, he was honoured to be on the top table, he had only been here three days, but he had been accepted straight away. Charles was saying they were being tipped off about an attack, but they were doing nothing about it. With the drone earlier he felt really at unease, he looked across at Mia, she was just looking at Charles, admiration in her eyes, perhaps it was being on his own for so long, but this was more like a cult than an association of any kind, it was clear that there was one leader, and that was Charles.

Charles' phone rang, this time he was expecting it, he

put his finger to his lips as if to shush the room, "Senator, what a lovely surprise, what can I do for you?" he asked as his smile beamed across the room, he liked being one step ahead as Illihad would be finding out soon.

Diana had sorted out the traitorous Senator by calling Charles first and informing him Illihad was going to call him with a bogus warning, telling him to flee the compound and vanish into the night, safely away before Raven could act. It was now time to sort out another issue, the double-dealing DEA guy, Gerald. He had tried to outsmart them, if anyone was an expert at double crossing it was her, she had worked too hard and waited too long for this day, she called in a kill team; another brave officer dying in the line of duty, a revenge target of a drug cartel most likely would be sad to hear on the news channels in the morning.

Marcus asked Mia to come to his bedroom as the room dispersed, he wanted to discuss the nights and days events, something was bothering him.

"What's up little brother?" she asked jovially, she had been in such a good mood since they had arrived, plus she knew she was due shortly, she rested her hands on her bump.

"This warning, I don't like it, doesn't it seem out of place to you?"

"Ah, calm down, you have been away too long, Charles

is connected, he had spies everywhere, we have helped a lot of these fools get into power, so they owe us. It's all good, I know it must have been hard for you, but honestly, Charles has it covered, there is no need to worry." She sat next to him, it must be strange for him to understand where they now stood in the world, it was true they had to live carefully, everyone had cameras on them now, information could spread around the world as soon as someone typed it, they had a good life as long as stayed near the head-quarters or had their wits about them, it must have been totally different for her brother alone for so long.

She patted his leg reassuringly. "Just relax, everything will be fine, we have a lot in place, we are just waiting for the right spark, the right incident to kick it all off, have a good night's sleep. Have you drunk today; you want me to send in someone?" she asked.

"Yeah, sure, that's a good idea," he smiled back, maybe she was right, perhaps a drink and a good night's sleep would ease his concerns. He felt bad wishing for simpler times, Mia left after she had called a slave in via the intercom.

Bina sat in her favourite yoga pose, the one she felt most at one with the universe, the Balasana. She was doing her utmost to prepare herself for the upcoming battle that was being carefully planned, it wasn't working, her mind would not settle, there was no way she was clearing her mind, emptying her thoughts today.

She had worked and trained all her life for this, stories had been handed down to her young mind, stories from way before her great grandad had ever encountered the Sages or whatever they were calling themselves at the time. The Jews had a chequered history with these enemies, like they seemed to have with so many races, but tomorrow she would be at the forefront of revenge.

She had been told of the siege of Masada, where a Jewish rebel leader, in fact a historian working for the romans had found out too much, he and his tribe had fled to the mountain fortress pursued by the roman army, he knew too much and it had ended in the mass suicide of everyone holed up in the ancient fort. As Judaism forbids taking your own life the history books have mixed views, some say a heroic standoff whilst others say a testament to extremism. Bina's mother had her own view, it was the work of the devils, simple as that.

The same thing had happened in York in northern England. Even after a thousand years not a lot had changed, an angry mob had trapped the entire cities Jewish community inside the tower of York castle, the mob was being used, wound up by the powers that be of the time, again rather than be murdered or forcibly baptised they had taken their own lives. It was no coincident in Bina's family view that this was the time of the rise of the Templars and their new allies' way down south.

She had grown up with these tales and stories, a reminder from history that her people had always had to fight for themselves, it certainly didn't start with the Nazi's and she suspected it wouldn't end with the death of the Sages, but she knew tomorrow would be a good start.

She gave up on the meditation, if she was to be on the top of her game in a few hours, she needed to get some sleep, though she didn't expect to get any.

Chapter Forty-One

2020 AD North Dakota

Marcus hadn't slept well, the thoughts just wouldn't go away, he had drunk well, the third time in as many days, he hadn't done that for years, maybe that had affected his sleep like when humans overeat spices or certain cheeses. Images of the glint in the sky, or drone as he believed it was, kept echoing and swirling around in his dreams. Surrounded by the smug look on Charles face as he had taken the call, coupled with scenes of Mia giving birth, not to a beautiful child but to a jet black feathered bird, eyes like his kind standing out against the darkness of his feathers, which was looking directly at Marcus, screeching a warning as it was held in her arms. 9/11, 9/11, 9/11 it repeated in a parrot like fashion over and over. As he awoke, sweating, he was now sure something was amiss. If Charles was so head strong on all-out war what made him think the enemy, who let's face it could be any nation, were not thinking the same way, plotting an attack on them? The set up here was great why risk it, in his view all of the people here, apart from the slaves, were way too complacent, an unhealthy mixture of naivety and cockiness.

He also wasn't so sure about the overall abilities of the tribe; they had had it too easy of late. Had they forgotten how hard the real world was? It was one thing sitting safe and sound in a group, all focussed on the task at hand, like a drone pilot bombing some target hundreds of miles away, all calm and collected, it was another having to function in the muck and bullets. It was only days ago he himself had been caught off guard and shot in the hand for his casualness. He liked to think the power was like holding a sniper rifle, it was great with no pressure, watching from miles away through binoculars, as your target went about their business, then a finger movement later they were dead. You wouldn't want a sniper's gun if they were bashing the door down just yards away from you, that was a different kettle of fish, you didn't have time on your side at all. If they were indeed attacked here, who would stand up and be counted, who could use their powers at the drop of a hat, under pressure, fighting for their lives? Who would come out on top? This place could be locked down like a modern-day fortress and power was in their numbers, that hadn't changed, but mankind had changed he feared.

The weather was minus four outside, no snow thankfully, that had stayed away. Still having an unending fear of doom from his nightmares and too much on his mind Marcus decided he needed to just get a breather away from the compound to clear his head, he wasn't used to so much company, he hoped Mia would come with him.

Snow was predicted and being thirty miles from the nearest store more supplies would be needed if they got snowed in, not for the main occupants but for the workers, they still had to eat and wash. When Marcus suggested getting away for a while Charles asked him, well told him really, to take the bus, along with some of the youngsters. Let them see a bit of the outside world, take them shopping, under his strict guidance along with five others. Although not happy, Marcus knew this was the only condition he would be allowed to leave, another reason why not to like this place, today it seemed more like a prison. It reminded him of Warwick castle back in England, beautiful, safe, as long as they followed the rules, Mia decided to stay behind, she wasn't feeling too good today.

The big yellow school bus was just another piece of the fleet they had acquired for personal use. Begrudgingly Marcus pulled on his seat belt and started up the bus as the twelve youngsters got on accompanied by four women and two men, he didn't recognise any of them. He insisted on driving as an excuse not to interact with them, they headed off down the lane.

Richard watched them leave on the screen from his vantage point miles away, this wasn't good, had they been tipped off, were more to follow? Panicked he checked the clock on the control room wall, the plane was scheduled in five minutes, the first strike of the planned attack.

No sooner had Marcus left, Mia felt the pain in her womb, a warning, oh no, her brother missing for over a hundred years had just left and now she was going to give birth. Not now she thought. She asked Charles to call her brother back as they took her deep into the tunnels to the medical centre.

As she laid on the bed a feeling of dread came over her, was this how every expectant mother felt just before birth? She looked at the faces of her nurses and realised it wasn't just her.

The pilot ejected, there was no stopping the jet now on its collision course. The news channels would report of an accident whilst on training manoeuvres, luckily hitting land in an abandoned area, the pilot bravely crashing his plane away from any schools or communities. No one would investigate why it had a real arsenal on board, or how big the explosion was, the nearest neighbours being over forty miles away were working for the attackers now.

Although no audio was in place Richard knew the complex had just gone boom, the feed from the drone turned into a fire and dust ball stopping anyone watching from seeing any details. Radio's crackled into life as the troops on the ground moved in; soldiers, engineers, fire brigade, amongst many others; most didn't have any idea who the targets were, terrorists they guessed. The ones with the guns knew no one was to be taken alive, no matter who came out of the buildings. Intermixed with the regular troops were Raven operatives, their role was to look for any tricks being played, make sure the men didn't turn their guns on each other or themselves, look out for illusions, anything paranormal, they all hoped the crashed jet would have taken out the bulk of the enemy. Looking around at what was still standing it had done its job.

Snipers had been placed in tactical places overlooking the area where they could, again kill on sight anyone, and that meant anyone, man, woman or child trying to escape. Most of these were Raven men and women, Bina was amongst the ground troops, she may have been older than most of the team, but she had looked after herself well and was as fit as she had ever been. Richard was back at the base helping run the show.

Mia was screaming on two fronts, physically by her body giving birth, mentally by her mind at the chaos unfolding around her. As with all of her kind such sudden death of so many hit them all hard in their brains, then the pandemonium in the tunnels amplified as they tried to work out what was going on, how they could fight back or escape.

Marcus felt the horror as he saw the plane fly overhead - way too low - seconds before a loud bang and a plume of smoke rose above the line of trees. He knew better than to turn around and go back, the inhabitants of the bus started crying, shouting and generally panicking. Marcus was the only one keeping cool, he knew they were the lucky ones. Pushing thoughts of Mia to the back of his mind, he put his foot down as he barked an order at one of the adults, they needed to get the hell away from here, anywhere would do but he guessed the back roads would be required, what had happened, what had Charles brought down on them?.

The snipers took out five people as they emerged from the now alight compound buildings, one armed with a machine gun the others unarmed, one even on fire, there was no different outcome as they were taken out with multiple shots before they could launch any kind of counterattack.

The troops on the ground were taking no chances as they set up a parameter. There was no sign of life as the building continued to burn in front of them, for ten minutes nothing happened as the fire fighters started to put out the main blaze to enable the troops to do a search inside for any survivors. The Raven agents made sure none of the regular troops lost concentration or relaxed, they knew the battle was not over yet by a long way.

All of a sudden out of nowhere, three people emerged to the left of the grounds unarmed, with their arms held up, not in a surrender position though. A nearby soldier turned and shot at the two men next to him making a small gap in the security line. The three ran towards this opportunity as a sniper took out the gunman, they were then gunned down themselves by other troops nearby, their failed escape attempt not making any ground.

The main fire was out now as they made their way into the buildings that were still standing, one man immediately started screaming, he dropped his gun and started swiping at his arms and legs "Get them off me, get them off me," as he rolled over trying to kill his imagined spider attackers.

"Keep moving" yelled an officer as another person helped the affected man, confused comrades looking at him as he acted so bizarrely.

The Raven operatives were expecting this, they hoped this was the highest level of resistance they would face, the plane taking out the majority of the enemy.

Bina was at the front of the troops as they found the blown open tunnel entrance, this was where it was going to get interesting, she and twelve men entered the tunnels, down the damaged concrete steps.

By now, Mia had given birth to a baby girl, Charles saw her being born, kissed her head and left, no time for sentimentality now, they were fighting for their lives, more than that, their very existence, it hadn't started well for the home team.

Chapter Forty-Two

2020 AD North Dakota

Richard had seen enough from the command centre; he was happy to leave the media team here working on the news channels and social media sites to cover up the plane crash. He was more concerned on that vehicle full of people who had left the compound just minutes before the strike. The command team were busy setting up roadblocks, but Richard knew that a bus load of Sages could easily use their powers to slip past any unsuspecting police officers. His thoughts turned to his partner and what she was now up against as they descended in further below ground, who knew what was waiting down there. He guessed that judging by the layout and facilities they had on ground level, the tunnels below would be equally impressive. The good news was the attack had gone well, any building left standing had been cleared and the feedback from Bina was that the tunnels had been at least half destroyed along with plenty of the enemy as they had passed body after body, a control room and nursery full of the dead.

He left and found his car, he was over two hours away on an airbase, he knew where he was heading, and it wasn't North Dakota.

Bina was at the front of a team of eight men, all similarly armed with machine guns and grenades, night vision googles and full armour. As they went down the steps she could hear the crackle of gun fire as the surface troops took out any targets in the remaining buildings above ground. The easy part was complete, it was now down to her and the Rangers team she was heading to do the rest. They had no idea who she was but were totally clear that she was in charge, she had already proved herself above ground. This set-up was weird, these men had previously taken on cartels in Mexico, insurgents in Iraq, terrorists in the mountains of Afghanistan, home grown threats, all manner of targets in totally different set-ups. What they saw here was something new altogether, however, they were experienced enough to know this was a special mission, crashing a fighter jet to start the day off told them that, coupled with the strange fight back. Seeing at least two comrades going mental made them think it was some sort of experimental facility, maybe mind bending drugs that a terrorist organisation was working on; having said that their leader, the small but capable woman was not wearing a gas mask; that made the men feel better, it wasn't air borne whatever it was. They moved tentatively further down into the only tunnel they could still access.

Bina estimated that over half of the entire network had been disabled by the first strike, that left a lower level that hadn't sustained too much damage. After a search of the top part, only coming across two more dead bodies in the stairwell, a bullet in the forehead to make sure, an act that looked to have confused her team they went down the stairs further.

Mia was still in the room, two nurses of her kind, the new-born and a human slave were with her. There was only the one door into this birthing room. After Charles had left they had cleaned up Mia and the baby as much as they could, Mia didn't personally know the people she now found herself with, but she knew they were not top commanders in the team.

"When was the last time you fed?" she asked.

"We are both full" one answered for them both as the other just nodded.

"Good, look, it looks like we are under attack, we need to get out of here, where are we, what level are we on?" Mia continued. She wasn't that good at the layout and had not taken enough notice as she was rushed to the birthing room that they were now trapped in.

"We are on level two, err, directly under the nursery and rest area. The vault is further down the corridor, then the stairs to level three, that's where the escape tunnel is."

"Okay" they all knew of the escape tunnel, it was part of their training and induction, the only thing on the bottom level.

It led three miles in one direction to an abandoned farmstead they owed on neighbouring land, that was it, no mono rail to an airfield just a tunnel, it had been put in when they first invested in the complex, no one really thought it would ever be used but this was where they were now.

"Charles is leading the fight back; we will be okay won't we?" they sounded as if they had total faith in their leader. Mia had found that most of the Sages here had only ever been in the village in Africa and then here in the compound, it seemed any outside tasks were for a talented few, ten to fifteen people that came and went.

"Yeah sure, he is very wise, brave, he will take them on, sure" Mia replied. She didn't believe it; she knew the only chance was to get to level three and run. "Come here" she beckoned to the human slave. After the birth she needed to up her strength, she wasn't planning on drinking him dry, she may need him for quite a while to come.

Charles was waiting to ambush the attackers as they came to level two, he wasn't sure who was left of his people, they had well and truly been taken out, it was a massacre. He had no time to dwell on this for now, he had to ignore his anger at his failure, he had to swallow his pride and admit he had been out played, so it was just him and Niles. Some tunnels had collapsed so it was tricky getting about, he had picked up a machine gun for each of them from the armoury and he was full as he always started the day with a drink. He knew he would need every last drop for today the way it was going, if this was the end he was going to make them work for it, he crouched down as he picked out some movement down the hall.

Bina edged forward, the lights were still working, a couple flickering on and off making the scene look very much like a video game. The man next to her had said about taking out the power, let their team have the advantage of night vision, a tactic they usually applied. She knew it would be of no advantage in this circumstance though, she stepped forward and felt strong arms grab her, holding her back.

"Shit" shouted the Ranger, he was staring at the hard-concrete floor by the final step, "You nearly fell down there" he said as he pointed at nothing.

How was there a wild running open drain rushing with water so fast down here he wondered, the plane must have caused this he thought as he looked at the illusion. He was about to think about the options on how they would pass this obstacle when the gun fire started.

Taking advantage of their enemies' confusion, as they paused; their concentration on not falling into the imagined hole and the ten-foot drop into the cold violent water, Niles opened fire. High powered automatic weapons were not his choice of arms, but he was proud he had hit at least one or hopefully two as they dropped to the floor, he dove back into the doorway to dodge the returning fire.

Bina ignored her comrades warning of the threat, she

knew as soon as he touched her it was an illusion he was experiencing; she didn't even see it herself; she even correctly knew it was a diversion and was diving for cover before the shots were fired. She fired off a barrage in reply before reloading, they had only just got to the level and one of her team was shot after falling for a trick of the mind, it was going to be a tough time clearing these last tunnels, she hoped her team were up to the task, she was now down to six men as one had taken the fallen comrade back upstairs. She threw an offensive grenade down the hall, the loud bang used to disorientate their prey.

Mia heard the gunshots then the explosion, she knew they were close, maybe as close as ten metres, she also knew she couldn't make a run for it, not yet, she had another plan, she needed the other two to help her if they were to stand any chance of pulling it off.

Marcus drove as fast as he could without raising any unwanted attention, he was so angry, why didn't he insist on Mia coming along? He had to remain in control though as he checked the sky for anything following them, watching them. With good luck they would be in Montana soon. Ivan, the only one of his new comrades on the bus that seemed to have anything about him suggested another safe house he knew of, over in Portland, it was nothing like the compound they had just left but it was well kitted out, maybe, he wasn't sure but there were some more of their kind there that could offer assistance.

Marcus knew they couldn't make that journey in one day, but he was sure there would be plenty of hiding places in the "Big Sky Country" as it was known locally. A good number of national parks and huge spaces would be their friend if they could evade any roadblocks, he was getting hopeful for their escape. He daren't think of his sister's plight; this attack seemed very organised, just who were they up against? Whoever it was had blindsided Charles, so much for his messiah persona, no time to dwell on that now, he had to get them all to safety first then look back.

Bina and her team edged expertly forward, they had shot another one who was half dead already but managed to crawl downstairs, the corridor was straight with rooms either side before it came to a crossroad, the men shooting had gone left. She stationed two of her team here as she and the remaining four slowly followed, this corridor was odd compared to the ones they had already passed, the layout so far had been quite uniformed, tunnel walkway, door to a room either side, each room six or maybe seven metres, this walkway there was no door on the right, something was amiss, the team stopped as Bina faced and inspected the wall.

Mia could feel the eyes burning into her projection, she was in two minds to just blow it wide open, smash the heavy metal door into whoever was outside trying to kill them, she decided to continue hiding, she and the two others all remained totally concentrating on keeping up the trick, she knew it was their only chance really, let them think this wasn't a room, there was no door, nothing to see here, let them move on.

Bina was unsure, she paced back to the junction then recounted the steps to where she expected a door to be, as she slowly raised her hand to the wall they suddenly came under attack.

Firstly the roof by the men at the junction gave way as pipes split and boiling water jetted at the men, they dropped to their knees screaming, this cut off Bina and the team who now came under heavy fire, one man dropped dead before Bina could even turn to the right direction, she dove on the hard cold ground once again as she used the fallen man as cover, she fired back as another Ranger threw a smoke grenade to confuse the enemy.

The noise in such a small space was intense, almost deafening, as bullets zipped past in both directions.

Knowing they were hemmed down the Rangers threw another smoke bomb and charged towards the gunfire, Bina followed them up, as she glanced back at the two men and collapsed roof to see if they were okay she saw the wall wobble, lose focus if just for a second, she knew it, there was a door there, after this fire fight she knew she would have to come back and find out who was hiding there, no time for that now as the enemy ran, one gunned down, shot in the back as he fled, they were onto them now the tide was turning as they were in hot pursuit.

The noise had gone, the fighting moved on, Mia grabbed

the boy and drank some more before pushing him to the nurse who had collapsed from her efforts, Mia didn't need any but wasn't sure when she would get the chance again, she was disappointed with the nurse; she must be very weak to be that drained that quickly. She grabbed her baby and listened at the door, gun fire was going off but a little further away now, it was time to go for the escape tunnel, it was do or die. "Come on, let's go" she commanded. They left the passed out boy and gingerly opened the door, stepping over the dead soldier, Mia picked up his gun as they passed him handing her baby to one of the nurses, she knew that was the best option, she wasn't impressed with her comrades, no wonder they just worked with the babies.

Charles was running, he was all out of ideas, he was lucky not to have caught a bullet like Niles just had, he dived through a door into the recreation bar room, his gun magazine empty, he was feeling drained in himself, he had cast two illusions, caused the roof to collapse, boil the water in the pipes before breaking them and scalding the two soldiers, he was running out of steam as well as ideas.

Bina and the three remaining Rangers burst into the room; they saw their target duck down. He seemed to take too long to do so, as he could have been hiding before they entered Bina thought. He knew they were coming, what did he have planned for them?.

Charles needed to see who he was up against for his last

throw of the dice, three well-armed SWAT men in the same uniform and a smaller person in front, must be the leader, a woman he guessed by her size, he searched for the weakest mind he could link into.

Bina was about to open fire at the bar as the man next to her dropped on her, she twisted as she too fell to the ground to see he had been shot point blank by his fellow Ranger. She then saw him alter his aim to her, as he shot her he himself was shot by the last man standing. It was too late as Bina felt her side erupt in pain, the shooter fell dead to the floor, the last man bent down to see Bina's wound, dark blood pumped out, he pulled off his helmet as he leant in to help her, a chair flew across the room knocking him out.

Charles himself fell face down on the floor on the other side of the wooden bar, he was spent, mind control to such an extent of making him kill people was tough going, then the telekinesis on the chair finally had done for him, he lay there exhausted hoping he had done enough so far until he had a chance to recover.

Mia heard the commotion as the tiptoed towards the stairs that led to the one place that could save them, she thought about going back, see if she could help but with the baby she now had other priorities. This place was done for, it was time to leave, get the hell out of Dodge as the saying went, the three of them with the baby went down the stairs and carefully and as quietly as they could opened up the last tunnel door, jamming it shut behind them.

They had done it, the road block for Marcus and his motley crew was easy going, the two hastily assembled traffic cops on this dusty road to nowhere were no match for seven Sages throwing up an image of a church outing, they saw the priest, nuns and catholic school kids all going to attend the choir contest over in the next town, nothing to see here, these aren't the droids they were looking for.

Bina remained conscious, she wanted to finish the job, stomach wounds always looked worse than they were she told herself as she pulled herself across the floor by one hand, leaving a bloody trail, the other held up a gun pointed towards where she had seen the man. If he came into view she was confident she could still take the shot, she was hoping he was in as bad a state as she was, if he was still okay she knew she was as good as dead. It took her ten minutes to claw her way to the side of the bar leaving a red smudge showing her short but painful journey, ready or not, this was it as she poked her head around the corner.

Charles was just starting to breath normally now, another couple of minutes and he would be able to stand, it had all been quiet, well nearly, he was sure he could hear something but wasn't sure what it was. He stood up to see the carnage, three downed troopers. Where was the female? he thought as his head turned slowly yet knowingly to the floor to his left.

Bina emptied her clip into the man before her as his shoulder was hit first making his body twist, then she hit his throat, cheek and ear as they all exploded in blood, bone and flesh. Charles was no more as his lifeless corpse hit the ground; it was the last thing the badly injured Bina saw as she slipped into unconsciousness.

Chapter Forty-Three

2020 AD America

Richard sat in the office and wiggled the mouse to make the screen jump back into life, it had gone to sleep as he had awaited his guest. Finally, CIA commander Diana Reagan joined the other eight Raven members in the room, she apologised for the delay, it had been a busy night.

"Okay, I want you to watch this" Richard began. He uploaded the CCTV footage from the garage and let it play.

A car drove in, they could see the woman they all knew now to be Senator Illihad get out, almost stumbling, her legs taking her somewhere her mind didn't want her to be. She was rigid in her movements as she took the hose off the pump, she then took over a minute as she entered something into the control panel; pay at pump looking the most likely reason. She proceeded to cover herself in petrol; the cashier seeing what was happening from his desk bravely ran out with a fire extinguisher; she set fire to herself, exploding into a fire ball. As flames engulfed her she appeared to panic in the last moments fighting what she was doing, she ran on fire around the forecourt for a good three minutes before succumbing to the flames.

The room was stunned into silence, Richard looked at them all before zooming out. "See this here?" he pointed to three by-standers who had watched the whole thing from across the courtyard. As soon as she lit up they calmly walked away.

"These are Sages, we know the late Senator was on the payroll. Thanks to Diana here we out foxed her, this here is payback for the betrayal, they must have put this in place before we attacked, or we could get to her. I think from her movements, her awkwardness, she was being forced somehow, mind control, however this proves one thing."

Most in the room knew what was coming, they let Richard spell it out so there was no confusion.

"We have the bus, seven or eight adults, we estimate as many as fourteen children, we have these three here, plus another three picked up on drone, one with a baby, escaping the compound. No matter how successful we were yesterday, we need to finish the job." he stated. The room remained silent as people viewed each other, it was Diana who spoke next.

"Okay, we need to shut down the country, limit any movement as we review the next targets, and find these god damn things. We can't let them flee into the night. Richard is right we are so close, we need to strike whilst the iron is hot, any suggestions?"

"We have been working on something, something that might work, at least for a while" said Helen Champion. She worked closely with the World Health Organisation, "We have been playing out a Spanish Flu scenario, we could, I think, if we can get enough people on board; the media, WHO, people in government; build this thing up that's happening over in mainland China. Get everything shut down until we find these things and wipe them out" she suggested.

This was big, was she saying they could close down the airports, the cities, lockdown the population, it couldn't just be America it had to be worldwide. They had stopped the planes before when they had needed to, not so long ago when the opportunity arose, but this was much, much bigger, however, they had never been this close before to finally winning.

"We have mapped dry runs on the computer for this, we have the blueprints for complete lockdown worldwide, the scripts are all written just need the blanks filled in" added another agent.

Everyone looked around the room, Diana was the only one with the power to give the okay.

"What's the name of this thing in China?" she asked.

"Err, hang on" Helen replied as she quickly checked her laptop, "Official name, COVID-19, it's a SARS thing we think, quite nasty but no Spanish Flu as of yet"

"Okay, let's do it, we have one chance people, those involved in this please leave and crack on with your plans, those that are focussed on finding our friends please stay here"

With that everyone left leaving Richard alone with Diana, "Sorry about Bina, I know you two are close" she said as she placed her hand on his shoulder gently.

"Thanks, she's strong, she will pull through, I can feel it" his face showing a sad smile. Bina was found near death in the depths of the complex, she had a life-threatening gunshot to her side, her team all but one dead. She was now in an induced coma as the surgeons had battled to save her life, it was touch and go whether she would pull through, she had done her job though, they all had as they counted and pulled the bodies out one by one. Apart from the three that they knew had escaped, there had been no other survivors from the attack, a job well done. Their prayers were with the families of the fifteen men and women who had given their lives for the cause, Diana wanted to ensure they hadn't died in vain as she swore they would take out every last one of the enemy.

Mia, her baby and her two companions had made it to an outhouse on the drug farming neighbours land. They rested the night there each taking turn on watch, the events of the day swam around their thoughts. The two "nurses," Nikki and Lucy, had never been out into the real world since coming to America, they were not the powerful leader type like Mia was. Sure they had the ability but they were more followers, they lacked ingenuity, initiative, gumpth, they could be of use but Mia knew the ideas and plan would have to come from her.

Whilst they slept she took time to take stock of what had transpired. It had looked so good, everything was in place, it worked, the humans were being nicely messed about with, divided upon any lines they could confuse themselves with, the final piece was in view, sure it was fifty years away, but still after all this time that was nothing to her. She thought back to the thirty years she had spent in Africa, laid up, at deaths door with the nuns, not even leaving that one room, not that she could have for the first twenty of them, now though it was nearly all gone. She needed to get to the nearest safehouse, away from here, they needed to make some distance, she knew if anyone was still alive the safehouse would be the best option. Nikki suggested giving Lydia a call, as she was out on a mission, Mia thought this a good idea. She wondered if Marcus know of this place, who was he with, surely they knew.

What a whirlwind of events and emotions it had been, finding her brother, the joy of showing their lifestyle, the attack, the birth, the deaths. She knew in her heart her baby was fatherless, she hoped he had died fighting. As the door illusion was fading she was sure she had felt his presence, she was sure it was Charles who had saved her by leading the attackers away, she would have liked to vow to honour his death by living and bringing up their child, right now she wasn't sure how she would do this. She had to think of a way to get away from this area, even this country, the humans would be all over it. She wondered if these two girls would stand up to be counted, in a way she was happy she was the out and out leader, she didn't need anybody questioning her authority or decisions as they fought for their very lives, the life of her new-born, tough times were ahead, she was in no doubt about that.

Chapter Forty-Four

2020 AD America

They had done it, amazingly the world was in lockdown. After an initial predicted panic, it had all gone better than they had expected, some countries were not playing ball but overall as Italy and Spain actually were hit with a huge amount of deaths the rest of the world, seeing their health system not being able to cope, all soon fell into line.

They had done what they had not thought possible. Richard wondered if anyone in that room a month ago actually believed they could do it, he never thought they could pull this off, but the virus turned out to be quite bad, or was he just believing their own lies and propaganda. The news was endless fear mongering as people queued, stockpiled, and then shut themselves away. What he knew though was his targets had been forced to stay where they were.

He now knew that the bus which he had seen leaving the compound had been driven by the man that had escaped him in

Vegas. They had crossed a roadblock in Montana, the reports from the two officers differed so much that it would have made funny reading if it wasn't so serious. One had seen a church outing, the other a travelling circus family, one vehicle, three vehicles, all women and children, dwarves and a bearded lady. It wasn't their fault.

Richard had been working on CCTV footage, and reports of anything strange since then, missing people, so far nothing concrete.

Bina was still in hospital but alive, that was good news, however, a full recovery was not on the cards. Richard thought about an office job for her, more like his role, it wasn't her thing really and who knows, they might both be retired after all this, it may have been a month since the fire fight, but he knew they were so close.

With the lockdown in place, the plane crash news came and went, no one was bothered about that. The bad thing with this massive lockdown operation in full swing, was the resources had been redeployed to help with the pandemic, that didn't help with the tedious groundwork of finding the last remaining Sages at large.

He didn't mind though, they were sure that the enemy was now just a handful in two of three states, they could not fly anywhere to safety, the net was closing in.

Marcus and his team had holed up in a hunting lodge complex, he was disappointed in the attitude of his comrades, they were so used to having everything on tap he feared for their future, this wasn't Charles' dream. These youngsters were as useless as their modern-day counterparts he thought, take the technology way from them and watch them fail. The generation of humans Charles had been working so tirelessly on influencing, he should have taken a look closer to home.

Marcus and Ivan had ventured out and found a family shacked up nearby, this was just before this incredible lockdown, but now they were running out of food for their captives. They needed to keep them alive to feed themselves, now a discussion was going on between the adult Sages.

"Okay, I get you are "Marcus" the oldest living one, well sorry after Mia, who happens to be your sister, oh and our leader's lover, but what puts you in charge?" Elsa said, showing how disgruntled she was with the situation.

"You know he is dead, don't you? Babock is dead" Marcus replied using Charles birth name.

"We don't know that."

"Yes we, do, come on, that place, all of it has been destroyed, it was a total attack, if we hadn't have left when we did we would be dead as well" Marcus argued, he felt it was falling on deaf ears though.

"I think we should make a deal" Elsa stated, "We are still useful, we have all these kids here, they must still want us, don't they?" she sounded delusional, a sad desperation in her voice.

"No way, they want us dead, gone, they flew a plane straight into our base, a fucking plane! Doesn't that tell you anything? I think this lockdown is about us as well, there has never been anything like this ever before, we wanted a war, well we got one." Marcus was stunned, a deal, no way, why couldn't they have just left it as it was, why were his kind obsessed with war as much as the humans had always been, maybe they weren't so unlike each other.

"Look, you are not in charge, we need to vote."

"Yeah, well vote without me then." Marcus huffed and got up to leave, this was going nowhere, he would rather be on his own again then work with these fools.

He went outside to the cold air hoping it would clear his head, Ivan had contacted Portland, they were still there awaiting instructions from Charles. There was a media blackout on Dakota, nothing was forth coming to shed any light on what the outcome of the attack was.

Marcus liked Ivan, he was the only one that had any sense, he had followed Marcus outside five minutes later.

"That was quick."

"Yeah, too quick, they want to hand themselves in, all of them."

"You, ……..you agree?" Marcus asked, not believing what he had just heard, had they learnt nothing!.

"No, that's why I'm out here with you" Ivan smiled. "Believe it or not I have seen this before, old Grigori, he and I had been sent to Russia at the turn of the century, see what was going on there, could they become involved or useful in the war effort, things were becoming bad, so off we went, we had been sent by Charles to cause some chaos."

"Grigori?" Marcus asked.

"Sorry, yeah, err, you heard of Rasputin, Grigori, that was his first name."

"Oh, I thought it was Ra Ra" Marcus replied trying to find some humour in their predicament.

"No, anyway we had travelled all the way from Africa to Russia, just the two of us, the humans called him the mad monk. I tell you they weren't far wrong, crazy times, anyway, let's take off, make our way west, I don't fancy dying here in the middle of nowhere, Elsa is a fool, always has been, meet me tonight, fuel up before we go, make it across the mountain and find a car. Let's go and find someone that can help us fight back." Both men looked into the distance at the snow-covered hills, it wasn't going to be easy going but no way were they handing themselves in.

They left that night, they didn't tell anyone, they wanted out before any calls were made to give away their hiding place of the last month. Elsa had convinced the others hers was the right plan, prove their value to the humans just like Charles' father had hundreds of years ago, a new beginning, it may have taken a long time, but she must have forgotten it hadn't worked out well.

Chapter Forty-Five

1916 AD St Petersburg

Ivan was liking his new name, the one given to help him blend in on his mission, he decided no matter what, he would keep this one, it was the trend with his people. When in Africa they all had kept their old tribal names, there had been no reason to change it, but the world, their world and more importantly their part in it had changed, it was time to keep up and take a more European moniker, his partner Grigori however had gone to the extreme, his back story was not what Babock had given him and nor were his clothes.

He had reinvented himself as a monk, a holy man from Siberia, Ivan had distanced himself as far away from him as he could, but had watched over him, he was on his own. Grigori had gone mad, he would have to kill him before he exposed everything and try and

They had been in this part of Russia for just over ten years, Ivan had watched his, literally, healed the Tsar's son Ivan was struggling to get anywhere near him. partner grow from wandering holy man, to church preacher, to society figure, he was so influential he was even part of the Tsar's court. Ivan knew he should have taken him out years ago, it would get back to Africa, as far as he had been told their presence had never been in this part of the world, no stories or events showed any evidence, but with the war on the horizon they were trying to cover all the bases.have been a lot easier for him then, but once he had magically

He knew his only chance would be to stoke the rumours that Rasputin was a charlatan, not this mystic, visionary prophet he claimed to be. Ivan needed to create, by helping discredit him, a chance to have him killed, get him out of the way, with no links to himself, so he could finally try and get back home. He knew he couldn't leave his ex-partner here in the eyes of man to be seen for what he really was.

Rasputin had become so embroiled into the court he had even been advising Tsar Alexandra himself on the armies, this had annoyed the generals and noblemen enough so that when the battles were going against them they struck. Ivan had been sleeping with one of the nobleman's wives, whispering thoughts, influencing her mind, that she forwarded on to her husband, seizing on Rasputin's unpopularity, he was assassinated by Ivan's lover's wife and a group of his co-conspirators, Ivan could now make his way back home to the warmth.

As he travelled south across the war torn countries, he

heard rumours of how hard it had been to kill his old friend, multiple gun shots, poisoned, stabbed and drowned, if only they had thrown him in the sea and not a river, then his body never would have been found. He knew he had done the right thing, staying there and making sure their secret remained, he knew Babock would be proud of him for sticking it out for so long, on his own but finishing the task in the right way, he never made it back to Africa as he diverted to America, finally meeting up another ten years later in New York, his name the only reminder of his time in Russia.

Chapter Forty-Six

2020 AD America

Mia, Lucy, Nikki and the as yet unnamed baby had slowly but more importantly made their way to Minneapolis. They had made contact with three others led by Lydia; they were now aware of the awful truth of what had befallen the entire tribe and about the few that were left. She knew her brother and another man were on their way to meet up with five rogue agents based in the west.

They were safe for the time being but as they watched the news they were well aware they were being hunted down to be killed, no deals would be made, the powers wanted no more from them although they still had allies.

The news reporter on the TV continued, "So, yes Dom, even in lockdown we have yet another school shooting here on American soil. A lone active shooter earlier today came back to this school, that is not confirmed I have to say, but early reports state an ex-student came on site, heavily armed and has killed five teachers and over, first estimates say as many as twenty children. Even in lockdown, this school was open for vulnerable kids, it's just so tragic. The enforcement officials are now closing the site off, I hand you back to the studio, this is Yevette Palmer signing off at yet another tragic school shooting here in Helena, Montana."

Mia couldn't be bothered to get up to turn the telly volume down, she lazily turned it lower with her mind.

"So" she began, "looks like Elsa's plan backfired." Once they had finally got in contact with her brother he had told them of Elsa's proposal. Watching the news, it looked like they had been ambushed, gunned downed, then a cover up staged. What did it say about this country that something like this could just be made up, nothing out of the ordinary with some gun wielding teenager shooting up a school, this proved to her though that their enemy was clever, powerful and above all else intent on wiping them out?

"This lockdown, that's them as well, obvious to me, they are stopping us from getting away," Lydia added.

"We need to join up with the others as soon as possible, power in strength, we are sitting ducks here on our own, we need a diversion, create some chaos, mask our escape, draw their resources elsewhere. We know that not all the agencies are in the know, they are being used, shutting down the world shows us they have a lot of power, able to influence a lot of people, but so can we, it's time to fight back. Let's put some of this stuff we have been doing over the years into place, it may be thirty years too soon, but what other choice do we have, all we need is a spark" Mia stated.

They all knew that Charles had been working towards a goal, a target, they had influence over many things, plenty of money which always helped, they had created division not just here in the states but everywhere worldwide, they all sat in their own thoughts thinking what could be done.

As they sat there the news continued with a breaking story, as they watched they all realised this had the potential to be the thing they needed, it was fight back time.

After the bus group had made a truce Richard ensured he was there after the massacre to do a head count. They had met under their terms to discuss a peaceful surrender, once they were all off the school bus they had been mowed down and then shot in the head. Resistance was attempted but failed, as the clean-up squad came in to take the bodies to the designated school where the stage was already set, Richard worked out that two adults were missing, a great day was now just a good day.

To anyone else it might seem odd that a stolen car was such big news in these parts, but Richard knew what was going on. The car was then spotted in Washington state on the 84, his quarry was on the run, he rightly guessed just the two of them now, these two weren't stupid enough to give themselves in. The enemies' size was reducing as riots exploded across the country and elsewhere to a lesser degree on the planet.

Richard saw through it, he felt this was the last throw of the dice, a smoke screen as they desperately tried to run for their lives. To him this was a good sign, sure lots of manpower that Raven could have utilised was now being used up in a different way, but it stank of panic, although it might help them to move about, there was still the lockdown, plus it would help him to move also. He was gunning for them now, he was doing it for Bina who sadly was still in a coma, he always thought this battle was personal, his family history intertwined, but thinking of his great, great, great, whatever grandad was nothing compared to how he now felt about his partner, they needed to die once and for all.

Chapter Forty-Seven

2020 AD Portland

Another month had passed so quickly, Marcus was nervous. At long last his sister was due to arrive today, along with his newly born niece, Ursula, named after their mother. It had been a mad time, maybe Charles had been right in his plan as the country had gone to shit, chaos reigned, the carefully laid plans over years and years of hard work had paid off as protests had kicked off in every major city over the death of someone in police custody, taking the learning from the Vietnam protests from the sixties they had lit the fuse throwing everything they could at it. The team he had met up with in Portland were great at their job, totally committed, they had sat there at their computers doing ten times more than anything he had seen in the short time he was in Dakota. They watched, fuelled, attacked everywhere they could, they didn't miss a trick, they financed transport, placards, they even had pallets of bricks and baseball bats delivered in bulk. The population had eaten it all up with riots every night. The government was crumbling, paralysed into inaction as fires and destruction reigned. The media completely confused reporting a blatant full-blown riot as a peaceful protest, paralysed with fear to say what was really going on, or using events as a political weapon, petty point scoring against one another in a time of crisis, it couldn't have gone any better as all resources that had combined to attack the compound not so long ago were now split up and diverted away, if only Charles had known how close they were he would have snapped at the chance. The fifty-year plan now looked out of kilter, he had lost the opportunity he had so looked for, planned for, perhaps he wasn't as clever as he had thought he was; however, it was the survivors saving grace at this particular moment as they regrouped.

With the lockdown being ignored for the riots, the confusion had enabled Mia and her team to cross the country to meet up today, they were to meet for the first time since the compound had been attacked. They may be only a few in comparison to Dakota but every one of them apart from the two nurses, Lucy and Nikki, and the baby were more than capable beings, the chaos outside could tell you that.

It was an emotional day for the siblings; however, they knew they couldn't dwell or celebrate for too long. Now, all remaining members were finally together they needed to seriously weigh up their options, Marcus knew he was most likely the only person that would like his idea, the others were indoctrinated into Charles' world plan, Marcus thought he knew better. He had played his argument in his head over and over once he had found out Mia was still alive, if she hadn't been on her way here he would have split, gone north, gone it alone again. Mia and the baby changed the game, he hoped she would see his side, come down on his side and back him up, if not he feared they were all doomed, they would all die here.

Richard couldn't believe the mass confusion and chaos that had enveloped the entire country, he thought his team had played the ace card with the lock down, that had been impressive, but now he felt they had been trumped by the enemy as night after night, protests and riots echoed around the world, people were being killed, buildings burnt, neighbourhoods trashed, statues pulled down, TV shows cancelled, history questioned, there was a lot of angry people out there and the enemy was using them well.

From having what seemed unlimited resource, a carte blanc cheque book, now they were just down to favours and the few Raven operatives, thankfully things had gone their way.

The one with the baby and her little group had been located, Richard had successfully persuaded his superiors to watch them and not attack. The lockdown enabled them to track them to where they were now, his hunch was right as they observed them meet up with what he hoped was all the remaining members of the tribe, here in Portland. That was how it had played out, all the pieces were now in the same box, that was the good news, the bad news being that this wasn't in the middle of nowhere like Dakota, this was in the centre of a city. They couldn't just out and out attack it, help from the regular agencies was sparse and the whole place was going nuts with protests and riots, protesters were even setting up their own roadblocks! The team following the targets had nearly lost them as they encountered a block on the highway. It was insane, these were just normal people who now acted with such authority they could block a major road with impunity. Richard even thought for one horrible moment that the people they were chasing, although only numbered five or six in strength had mind controlled the whole lot of the crowd, that was a lot of people, he was starting to wonder if they were that powerful, he thought better of it and put it down to the brain washing and indoctrination over the years rather than an instantaneous trick from his prey knowing they were being followed. His better judgement told him it was just these self-righteous Antifa lot, they were so full of confidence and they were experts at whipping up an angry mob, Richard knew where their funding came from though.

So, this was it, the enemy had been reduced to just a handful, a powerful handful, that fact needed to be at the front of their thoughts for any plans they had, holed up in an apartment in the city centre. The element of surprise had been played, successfully so, it had to be said, but that was then this was now, Richard looked around the room at the other five Raven agents, good experienced men, no women on the team this time he noted, much like it was in his ancestors day.

As he waited for the call from Diana he took the time to think back to his ancestors all those years ago as they had hunted down the England based Sages, this is what it must have been like for those brave men, no technology to help them against a magical foe, just guts and balls, going toe to toe with someone that could throw anything at you and all you had in return was your wits and your gun, no drone support, no radio communication, no CCTV, it must have been hard as much as it was scary, just like now. He looked back to what his family had achieved for inspiration for his own situation right now, he recalled a story of his great, great whoever, uncle Matthew something, he had led some of the first attacks. As the generals had realised that someone inside wasn't happy and sticking to the plan of continuing to use the Sages for the good of the empire, they had placed the asset in the sea fortresses near Plymouth for three reasons, one, help stop Napoleon invading, two, to keep them safe from the internal enemies, thirdly if they went rogue they would find it pretty hard to escape being surrounded by all that salty water.

It hadn't worked, Matthew had led a small team to each fortress, braving the cruel sea in their little boats and took out each target as well as the men guarding them. He was seen as a real hero for his deeds, this was now how Richard needed to be, brave, focussed and most importantly successful, he was more than aware that he was the last of his line, him being the only boy and he sadly hadn't passed on the family name, his part would have to be the final downfall of this centuries old foe.

The call came through, with what was going on. Diana could only spare another ten troopers, a single SWAT team. If they could wait, but she couldn't say for how long, when things settled down she could commit more, right now that was the only offer, take it or leave it.

Richard knew the window of opportunity was closing, the targets weren't going to just sit around waiting to be caught no matter how well their plan was going, this was it, they would attack tonight.

Chapter Forty-Eight

2020 AD Portland

Marcus was holding his cute little niece, Ursula, he had been expelled from the meeting as things had got heated. He had gone to get some fresh air on the roof garden of this rather nice apartment, this was typical of their brashness he thought, another fantastic venue, everything in place including a nicely stocked fridge full of blood containers of different sizes, no need to go out to find food for quite a while yet, it wasn't as good as straight from the vein but it would do, however, to Marcus this place summed them up. It was way too in your face to remain in the shadows he thought, no subtlety these days, this swanky downtown apartment had Charles' arrogance stamped all over it.

    He had fallen asleep with Ursula on his lap, dreams invading his mind once again, this time it was the school bus, but he wasn't driving, the sparkly eyed raven was, as it cackled away at him, he was the only one on the bus and it looked like they were heading into hell, flames licked the side of the vehicle as the bird repeated, "inferno, inferno, inferno."

Marcus woke with a start, he checked his watch, he had only dozed off for five minutes, but it seemed a lot longer as he recalled his latest nightmare, he started thinking about what had been discussed downstairs and if they had got anywhere nearer to a decision.

Half the room thought things were going well, no need to do anything different to what they were doing, sit tight as the enemy tore themselves apart, that was the plan all along, they wanted to see out the plan, honour the fallen by seeing it through. Marcus had explained it couldn't last forever, they had to use this smoke screen and escape, get away to the expanse of Canada, hide out, disappear, while they still could. Did they really think this uprising, no matter how unbelievably well it was going so far, could last? No, it would inevitably implode, when the weather changed, that always seemed to be a protests nemesis, no one liked rioting in the wet. Defund the police, how would that play out, no matter what mixed messages the team here were flinging about the silent majority were indeed that, still the majority. The protesters were enjoying their moment in the sun but they should know, they were all old enough and ugly enough to know these things always ended. The French revolution, once all the aristocrats were dealt with the generals simply moved into their chateaux's and picked up where they had left off; the Tsars replaced like China's emperor with high ranking party members; it was the humans nature, no matter what good intentions started any cause, redistribute the wealth, free health care for all, whatever, someone had to be in charge, and once they got the power they were hell bent on keeping it, normally more so than those they had just taken it from, no matter how humble their beginnings. It had got heated so he had left, he thought that was best.

Mia was starting to see her brother's point in all this, she felt that certain members were purposely ignoring him simply because he was a newcomer, an outsider, someone looking to take over from Charles, she knew he just wanted to live his life, tired of the endless fighting and running.

Most wanted to stay here, they felt safe, they wanted to continue spreading the poison, create the chaos, use the lockdown against the enemy, increase confusion with contradictory facts to destabilise the government, not just here but worldwide. It was all for the taking, from here, this set up they could continue to interfere, ease lockdown, enforce lockdown, falsify data, cripple economies, help point the finger of blame, mixed in with the protests this thing could go on forever, the news channels were already talking about 2021, strike whilst the iron was hot.

The SWAT team were ready and in place, three Raven agents including Richard were with them in the cramped van as they headed to the apartment block, the remaining agents in strategical places nearby in case of any issues or escape attempts, they too were preparing to strike.

As the team made its way there and the Sages continued to argue. Marcus was watching in interest as little fires now lit up the night sky along with flashing blue lights. It looked like the protests were coming closer to home as he saw the federal building opposite being hastily re-boarded up where the heavily graffitied fences had been previously smashed down in part. He shook his head at the foolish humans as the noise increased and he could hear the chants, screaming and counter arguments, of all the things he had seen, had experienced before over literally thousands of years, this as the humans would say "took the biscuit." These people lived in such a great style these days, he had seen such death and disease, war upon war, he knew millions still lived in poverty, proper poverty, not just poor like in this land but some lived horrible lives, what did these idiots actually want he wondered as he spotted the inconspicuous looking van turn the corner and pull up outside their apartment, he ran back downstairs as quickly as he could.

He wasn't the only one to spot the van, the lady with the loud haler had too. Fearing they were about to get stomped on, she made the gathering angry crowd aware of what she had seen as she directed a group to interfere with whatever the men in that van had turned up for, the federal building was surrounded as she watched, she could spare some of her soldiers to make sure the task tonight wasn't stopped, this place was going to fucking burn, fuck the police.

As the team exited the back of the van they were

surprised to be confronted by a gang of youths running towards them, this wasn't part of the plan, a bottle smashed against the door shattering glass over two men, they were in full riot gear so there was no affect, Christ thought Richard, as if they didn't have enough on their plates tonight already.

Marcus shouted, "They're here" as he entered the room. Nothing had changed since he had left, they were all still debating their options, well their choices were now limited he knew.

You could see the panic in the eyes of the younger members, it was all well and good sitting back, causing death and destruction from a safe distance, they had learnt nothing from the recent attack, they would all see now who would stand up and be counted, who, away from a computer screen was any use in a fire fight. A ground soldier versus a bomber pilot, the pilot may have the skills but it was different when you could see the whites of their eyes, Mia ran towards Marcus and took Ursula from him, Ivan and two others went to get some guns, whilst Lydia rallied the remaining clueless ones including Nikki and Lucy to form a circle, they began praying. Mia wondered what spell Lydia had in mind, she had shown she was one of the most powerful ones in the room, even matching Mia, she thought about joining them helping out, but she for once was caught in two minds as she held her baby, what she was sure of though, was that this wasn't good.

The SWAT agents looked to the other men for instruction, they had been briefed of a terrorist threat, a proper full on nasty one perhaps even a dirty bomb, therefore no matter what, follow their orders to the letter, no matter how harsh, they formed a line against the approaching angry pumped up crowd as small missiles landed around them.

Richard looked at the entrance to the apartment, two of his men were attaching the small explosives required, he looked back at the baying crowd, he didn't have time for this. He was sure the Sages upstairs were aware of them by now, they were losing any advantage they had, god knows they might even be mind-controlling these idiots down here as they plotted their escape, he took his side arm out and shot the nearest protester squarely in her face, the expelled blood matching the colour of her hair as she dropped to the floor, just for a moment the crowd fell silent, before turning and running.

"Come on" Richard said as he turned towards the door that had just burst open, "you five stay here and safeguard our escape, any trouble kill them, anyone but us comes down take them out too, the rest of you follow me." He continued taking the lead, this is what he had been waiting for, this is what Bina would have done, take the bull by the horns, no more messing about, he was doing it for her as much as anyone else, her condition would not be just another pointless pawn in the war, they entered the building.

The crowd wanted vengeance, seeing someone gunned down though had altered their thinking, no one was taking on the heavily armed men parked outside the apartment block, everyone stayed well back across the street, the shouting had now continued as a lot of people were not sure what had gone down, rumours were rampant and everyone could see the body but were unsure of the exact details, some had, without a hint of irony phoned the police to come to their aid, the sirens now could be heard getting closer.

The woman on the megaphone, unaware of the shooting, directed their anger on the federal building as petrol bombs were thrown, placards set on fire and anything else combustible was mounted up, the feds were going to pay.

Not daring to take the lift, completely aware that the enemy knew they were there, Richard carefully led the team up the stairs, totally ignoring that it looked like it was on fire. The Raven men knew to expect this, the SWAT team not so much, but they followed up, confused as the fire firstly didn't affect the men in front of them and to their joy them neither.

The Sages had blockaded the door with every bit of furniture they could manage, the three with guns placed to take out anyone that entered. Marcus knew it wasn't enough, he ran to the kitchen, grabbed two small flasks of blood before he grabbed Mia, who was holding Ursula, and bolted for the roof top garden, he hoped the others would put up a good enough fight, even win, buy them enough time to escape somehow, to enable their getaway. His arguments and advice had fallen on deaf ears, they were all believers in the cause. The master plan their deceased leader had programmed into them, he half believed even now with what had happened recently, they still thought they could win, take over and rule the world, they were superior to the humans and that just how it should be, they would never live as he had, taking what blood he needed and just letting them get on with it, it was to be their down fall, hopefully not his.

The crowds were getting braver, the building was slowly catching fire, the cops had turned up and were standing off against the SWAT team in a bizarre twist. The protesters hurriedly telling them what had happened to the dead girl, showing them any footage, they had, a camera crew had turned up, the whole situation was weird, total pandemonium, even by the last months standard.

The SWAT team left downstairs were unsure what to do, they were just about to lay down their guns to the city cops when some black SUV's pulled up, Diana Reagan stepped out amidst twenty CIA operatives, guns already drawn backing up the five men. No one apart from Diana really knew what the hell was going on, CIA, SWAT, local police, rioters and protesters alike, it was mayhem.

The door to the apartment was blown, a mix of grenades thrown into and through the assembled blockade of chairs, tables, beds and cabinets, smoke filled the room as gun fire exchanged, one Raven agent succumbed to a mind trick as he just walked straight forward into the melee, dancing, looking like he didn't have a care in the world, he dropped down dead. Richard unsure which side shot the fatal bullet. His team had advanced in just a little bit as cutlery and pans hammered down on them, a big carving knife taking out another man as it had sailed through the air. He rallied his men as they now moved behind cover in the large open planned lounge area. This place was very nice he thought as the enemy gun fire seemed to be running out, he did a quick head count, he saw three SWAT team, one of his team and himself, the radio crackled, more men were coming up the stairs, good, he knew Diana wouldn't let him down, when it counted, or let him take all the glory was more like it. She was a very capable but ambitious woman; he wouldn't put anything past her but he was glad she was on his team.

Marcus knew they were trapped, the blazing battle downstairs was coming to an end, instead of hearing sustained shooting it was now organised pot shots, he knew which side were doing that, he looked at his sister, searching for inspiration, "Any ideas?" he asked.

Mia had one, she had seen it used once before, but that was only one person, a very old wise and powerful Sage, a woman she had known, ages ago back in France. She had become trapped as the castle had collapsed, separated from the others with the enemy closing in, teleportation her last-ditch attempt for safety, it was a rare a spell as foresight was and it was very draining. She looked around, over the edge, the place was crawling with people now, she instructed Marcus to stand on the edge, her plan was to send him over the road to the nearest safe building she could see, then he would have to help her and Ursula join him, she wasn't sure if he could do it on his own but if he could join her thoughts, concentrate on that it just might work.

"I can't leave you again, I just can't" he screamed as his body jolted and was magically transported over to a big building opposite, he fell over as he landed, he dusted himself off quickly and jumped up to visualise his sister, join her mind to help her, he didn't know how she had done what she just had but he knew it was the last throw of the dice.

The sages had played their tricks, taking out two more SWAT men making them turn their guns on each other, this worked against them two ways, Richard knew this mind control was incredibly power zapping, leaving the enemy flat out, they would be struggling now to stay awake never mind fight, secondly the remaining SWAT man had gone mental in his own way and dealt with it by bravely charging straight at the last of them, he was going down fighting. His superior guns and skills making mincemeat of the remaining, exhausted Sages, his man was now coup de gracing the bodies as Diana came in, she looked around the battle zone.

"Where's the baby?" she asked

"Two made a run for it, I'm on it" Richard replied as he bounded up the stairs, he was so close now he let his caution fly in the wind, that's what Bina would have done.

Mia, after seeing Marcus land readied herself and started the spell again, it had nearly gone to plan but she saw he was on the wrong building, this one was busy being set on fire by the angry mob below, they would have to cross that bridge when they got there, first things first get off this roof, it may be on fire over there, but she hoped it would be a safe haven long enough as she recuperated her strength. The good news was it didn't look like their attackers would stand a chance of raiding that place, not with all the protesters and the fire taking hold, she was ready, she could feel Marcus in her mind.

Bang, Richard shot her in the back as soon as he clasped eyes on her, taking out her left shoulder, she dropped Ursula to the ground as she reeled from the pain and turned towards her shooter.

"Noooooooo" Marcus screamed, he not only saw her twist as the bullet ripped through her but being linked he felt the actual physical pain, but it was nothing compared to the emotion, a force erupted from him like nothing he had ever felt, maybe because of the power she had been focussing on, but somehow he teleported her to his side.

They both collapsed out of sight on the roof of the burning federal building, both completely exhausted, with Mia suffering a bad gunshot wound as well.

Richard couldn't believe his eyes, she had vanished, in all the books he had read, in all the stories he had been told, never had he heard of this ability, he looked around to see if she was anywhere close by, still on the roof, was it an illusion, yes, that was what it must be, his eyes darted side to side as he quickly made his way to the baby. If it was an illusion she would be back for the baby. Although it had been dropped when he took the shot it looked okay, unharmed, apart from crying, it wouldn't be soon he thought as he held his pistol against her soft dark fluffy hair. If he was attacked it would be dead, he saw Diana come through the door with three bodyguards, good re-enforcements he thought.

Marcus lay next to Mia, he was done for, he was just lying there, his breathing heavy, no strength to even put his arm around her, totally drained, he could hear her sobbing, she had lost her baby, she had waited over two thousand years, and now she lay there, as useless as he was, drained of all of her power, trying to escape and failing, totally failing. She looked like she did that day on the ship, lost, finally beaten, she had had enough, this was to be the end, the real end this time. They could both feel the heat rising below them, neither even having the strength to stand up, never mind cast a spell, do something useful, they could hear the crowd outside cheering above the noise of sirens and the anarchy as the fire took control, they both managed at the same time to move their heads and look at each other for one last time, this was the end Marcus knew it, not just of his life, which to be fair had been incredibly long, even by his own peoples standards but for his entire people, he knew the others they had just left downstairs were all dead by now, Ivan, Lydia, even Ursula, all dead.

The humans, they just couldn't live together, it could have been so good if it wasn't for the leaders, on both sides it had to be said. Charles was sure that he needed to kill over nine tenths of the world, to rule over them, as the humans themselves wanted to wipe each other out all the time as well as the Sages. Their history was so bloody short yet that's what it was, bloody. It was true, just like the rioters down stairs, the ones that his kind had manipulated into this latest class war without them really knowing, they thought history was a lie, told by white supremacists, certain people had been written out of it, the irony that it was a fire that Charles had lit had literally led to these actual real flames that was now to be their end, not the people chasing them trying to kill them, it was laughable as it was poetic. The flames were now visible on the roof top as the whole building was a blaze, the heat intensifying, yes history was a lie, the past was being rewritten as great men of history, their past deeds and lives were now questioned, no one was safe as statues were torn down, books and philosophy reviewed, everything was being questioned and held up against modern thinking, the future, who knew where this runaway train was heading, as he lay there finally dying, all out of ideas. What he did know was that his kind was leaving a present that day, a present that no one had ever really asked for.

Diana picked the now crying baby from Richard's dead arms, it looked so human, even more so now it was bellowing, if you didn't know then it was really hard to tell. The bright blue eyes looking back at her, Richard wouldn't have understood, that was why he had to go, his proud family history would have insisted that every last one of their enemies were dead. She felt bad as her guard expertly stabbed him in his spine, the look of shock on Richards face as he stared at her, he had just about to say something but she didn't have time to stop the pre given order, perhaps it was nothing, as his mouth moved up and down emitting no words, his eyes telling their own story oh well, "needs must when the devil drives" she thought. She would tell his uncle he died fighting the good cause, in the line of duty, they couldn't have done it without him, she consoled herself that most of it was true.

He had been a good man, a fantastic agent, he had been instrumental in getting them all here today, no one could deny that, but he had a closed mind, he couldn't see how important this baby was, the powers these being's possessed, no, this little one needed to be cared for, alright it had a few years in a lab first. Diana had heard that they were babies for ages, she knew herself that she wouldn't be around when the asset reached a useful age, but she knew she would go down in history, a CIA legend, that was her legacy, the one that tamed the beast, brought peace to the world she hoped, it didn't seem like it as the smoke swirled into the reddened sky, the braying crowd cheering as the building collapsed, seemingly already forgotten about their fallen comrade, but she knew, now Charles and his meddling were out of the way, normal order would resume, the peasants would be stopped from revolting, like they had so many times before.

Acknowledgements

I hope you enjoyed my version of history, horror and folklore.

A big thank you for the cover artwork to David at dccovercreations.com. The picture used was a photo I took in Cambodia whilst visiting a silk farm, on one of those day trips that you can get involved in when abroad.

I hope I explained the reason for this cover in the story with Marcus's analogy on how he feels his people were treated.

My inspiration for this novel was a book I got one Christmas titled "All the countries the English have invaded and a few they haven't." It got me thinking how a small island off the coast of mainland Europe punched above its weight for so many years, the sun never setting, and all that stuff associated with the Empire. Was something helping or pulling the strings from behind the scenes?.

Mixed with my love of history, horror, suspense and pop culture my story gained its own life. The novel you have just read being the fruit of all this.

Thank you for downloading it, I hope you enjoyed reading it as much as I did writing it, and don't worry, it's not true, honest!

Afterall, His story is a lie.

Printed in Great Britain
by Amazon